CURSE OF THE OROCHI

The Dragon Within Book II

David Angelo

SPECIAL THANKS

I would like to thank my editor, Marissa Taylor, for helping me to proofread and edit this novel. Please check out her website at www.ataylorededit.com.

CONTENTS

PROLOGUE

オロチのバラッド

(The Ballad of the Orochi)

Long ago, in the foothills of Mount Sentsu in the Japanese province of Izumo, there lived an old couple named Ashinazuchi and Tenazuchi. The couple lived with their eight beautiful daughters along the banks of the Hii River, where they grew rice and brewed their own unique brand of strong sake. Together they lived in harmony for many years, until one fateful day the hills around Sentsu opened up and an eight headed dragon called the Yamata no Orochi emerged. The beast had scales of the deepest green, eyes as red as winter cherries, and a roar that parted the clouds. The creature descended on the family and consumed one of their daughters, before departing back into its mountain lair. It returned the year after to consume another daughter, and the following year a third. By the eighth year, the couple had lost all their daughters, save the beautiful Kushinadahime. As the day of her death drew near, Kushinadahime clung to her parents, lamenting the life that was to be cut short.

One day a brave warrior named Susanoo found himself walking along the banks of the river Hii when he came upon the grieving family. Susanoo became smitten by Kushinadahime, and promised to kill the Orochi in exchange for her hand in marriage. Kushinadahime obliged, and together they filled eight jars with her family's signature sake, which Susanoo carried to the mouth of a large cave where Orochi slept. The clever warrior told Kushinadahime to hide.

Then, he waited.

The Orochi emerged from his cave and stopped in front of the sake. After inhaling the pungent fumes, the eighth and smartest of the heads declared it was an offering made to them, and they all plunged into each of the jars and drank of the sake. When the jars were licked clean, the Orochi lumbered along the edge of the mountain, barely able to stand upon its talons. As the creature readied itself to prey upon the family, Susanoo pounced. He sparred with the Orochi throughout the night, hacking off the heads one by one, until finally he delivered a mighty swing and struck the eighth head near the base of its spine. His sword shattered, and the creature fell.

With the Orochi dead, Kushinadahime emerged from her hiding place and she and Susanoo embraced. But Kushinadahime noticed something shiny protruding from the severed neck of the eighth head. She pointed a dainty finger at the thing, drawing Susanoo's attention. It was the hilt of a sword, covered with blood, glimmering in the light of a summer dawn.

He grasped the *tuska*, and drew a blade of the whitest white, a blade so beautiful that he immediately presented it to Kushinadahime as a token of his love.

Susanoo and Kushinadahime were wed, and the sword that was pulled from the neck of the Orochi became known as the *Kusanagi no Tsurugi*. It resides today in a shrine, hidden from all, except from the eyes of the Emperor himself. And the Yamata no Orochi was never seen or heard from again.

Or was it?

オロチの呪い

竜の内部 ブック II
デイヴィッド・アンジェロによって

CHAPTER 1

Nicole Newheart awoke sometime around dawn. Blue light pouring from the window above the bed, and the gentle hum of traffic intertwined with the chirps of birds greeted her ears. Nathan was still asleep, his messy patch of blond hair sprouting from the top of his blanket. Nicole smiled and sank deeper into bed, pulling the covers up to her neck and watching as the morning light danced across the ceiling. She had forgotten how quiet the outside world was compared to the tunnels, whose atmosphere was disturbed by the roar of trains and the squeal of rats. It made her wonder how, and why, she had tolerated it for so long, and why she hadn't done more to experience this little slice of heaven that so many took for granted.

Nicole was just a girl when her mother sent her off to protect her from her father and the horrible plans he had for her. She had spent her formative years in the tunnels beneath New York, unable to live the life of a normal teenage weredragon, or what could be considered normal in an existence so fraught with violence and strife. Ten years, ten long years hiding from her father, Lucio Salvini, and her brothers, who wished to exploit her for their dastardly means. The men of her family were a violent, sadistic group of dragons, heads of an empire of crime that used fear to achieve its goals in the name of total domination. In their eyes, Nicole was a golden ticket, a commodity, a toy from which they could derive both pleasure and pain. Lucio himself thought she was key to overthrowing human civilization, but only if she slept with one of her siblings in exchange for a powerful heir. It was a fate her mother, Chyanne Newheart, could not bear, and when the time came, she faked Nicole's death and hid her underground.

As punishment, Chyanne was sent off to Hong Kong, a country where no one spoke her language, separated from her daughter and everything she knew and loved. Seeing no way to escape, Chyanne had taken it upon herself to end her suffering, if only to save herself and her daughter from Lucio's wrath. When Nicole learned her mother had taken her life, the world around her became a little darker, a little colder. She had resigned not to live, but to simply exist, to move through life on autopilot, to let the world turn without her and without so much as a passing glance. To drift from one wasted day to another, until she met her fate at the claws of an adversary or by her own.

Until now.

She imagined what her mother would think of her now, lying naked in bed next to the young man who lit the match that brought the light back into her world. She loved Nathan Van Cleef, loved all the little ways he brought the best out of her. She loved his courage, his compassion, his bravery. She admired his dedication, and the way he put himself in harm's way for others. Nathan was the one who stood up to Lucio when no one else did, who sparred with her siblings and foiled their plans, and who plunged a stinger full of venom into her father's neck and dropped him off the edge of the Empire State Building. In the course of two weeks, Nathan had helped to end the war her father had waged for centuries, and ushered in a new era of peace for all weredragons.

But the battle in lower Manhattan had brought with it scars of its own. Nicole remembered the long days she had spent with Nathan, sifting through the rubble of 432 Park Avenue, looking for any signs of life. The building had been lit aflame when Lucio and his men torched it with their fiery breath, causing the massive tower to buckle under its own weight and collapse. There were times she felt hopeless, when the bodies of those they had failed to save began to pile up. But then Nathan would hoist her up and share a word of encouragement with his family's brand of optimism that she found intoxicating, and she would keep going.

She recalled how they had made love last night, and thought of quickening, the moment a female weredragon chooses to become pregnant. She could see herself with Nathan for the long haul and could see her having his children. But then she thought it rather cruel and foolish to have a child before either of them was ready. And so, she vowed to let his seed die within her and put off motherhood for at least a little while.

As she sank deeper beneath the covers, Nicole let her thoughts consume her as she pondered all the people in her life and where they fit in her head. There was Seth, her surrogate father, and the wisest weredragon she knew, whose knowledge and experience was immeasurable. There was Joel, Seth's buddy by circumstance, whose optimism kept her going during times of need. There were Nathan's aunts, Tiffany and Tina, his grandpa Lionel, and his uncles Simon and Toby. There was Eugenia, the leader of the DC Sanctum, who had given her a large check in exchange for helping to end her father's reign. And of course, there was Nathan's mother, Marjorie. She was the only non-weredragon Nicole knew on a personal level, and she was about the nicest woman in the world. The fact that she had lent her a place to stay after the battle was enough for Nicole to love her for all eternity.

Then there were those in her life she did not love as much. Her brother, Lucca, the man her father wanted her to marry to keep their family bloodline pure. There was her sister, Delany, who had bullied and mocked Nicole throughout childhood for her indigenous blood. A small, sadistic side of her savored the final look on Delany's face when she was shot down and splattered across half of Times Square.

Then there was her father, Lucio, the man she hated more

than anyone or anything. Watching his final, painful moments was more satisfying to her than sex itself. She got goosebumps whenever she recalled how he begged her to save him, and the look on his face when she refused. It was a look of despair, of shock. Even after all the pain he had caused her, Lucio still expected her to serve him. Good riddance.

If a hard life taught her anything, it was to compartmentalize those she loved from those she loathed, like how a grocery store determines what to keep and what to throw away. She knew some people wouldn't understand or think it cruel or callous to treat others like they were disposable, but she knew if she forgave them all, she would open herself up to more pain. Nicole's forgiveness was something earned, and it came gradually. It didn't happen overnight. And not even she knew how long it would take, or if it would happen at all.

As the glow from outside changed from blue to amber and the sound of traffic began to pick up with the morning rush, Nicole accepted the fact that she wasn't going back to sleep. She got up, pulled on a t-shirt and a pair of Nathan's gym shorts, and made her way to the bathroom. When she finished her morning ritual, she walked downstairs to the kitchen and poured herself a glass of water. As she maneuvered around the Van Cleef's small kitchen, she noticed her burner phone had a missed call. She glanced at the screen and saw the call was placed around seven the night before, when she and Nathan were busy with other things. There was no number, but the caller ID said that it was from Hong Kong SAR. Nicole narrowed her eyes and looked at the screen more closely. She found there was a voicemail message attached. She unlocked the phone, expecting it to be nothing more than a scammer or a wrong number. She sipped her water and tapped the message.

"Um, hey Nicole," said a shaky female voice. "It's. . . it's Mommy."

Nicole froze, the glass half touching her lips.

"How. . . how are you?"

Nicole started to tremble. She knew this voice, had grown

to crave its sound when she was a little girl and had learned to imagine it during difficult times. There was a long pause, during which the voice seemed to hyperventilate like someone having a panic attack.

"I'm going to come see you," she blurted out. "I'll meet you in New York, and we can talk about it all. I love you, Nicole. See you soon."

The message ended. Nicole placed her glass down and stared at the message. There was no way this was a prank or some kind of trap; that was her mom's voice and her voice alone. Nicole clenched her chest and began heaving. She sank to the ground and planted her back in the corner between the stove and the sink. She looked at the message with tears in her eyes, her brain full of conflicting emotions. She was happy and angry and sad all at the same time. She tapped the message again, listened to it, let her mother's voice soothe her. She tapped the call back button and waited for a response, but it ended without a dial tone. A metallic voice told her the voicemail box had not been configured. She placed the phone next to her, buried her head in her hands, and trembled.

"Nicole?" Nathan asked. "What's wrong?"

She pried her hands away from her eyes and saw Nathan standing over her, wearing nothing but his boxers. He knelt and brushed strands of black hair from her face as she took her phone and played him the message. After listening, he sat down next to her and placed an arm around her shoulders.

"It's her," Nicole said.

"Are you sure?" Nathan asked. "Could this actually be her?"

Nicole nodded. "Yes. The tone, the dictation. It's just the way she talked."

"She said she's coming to New York," Nathan said. "From where, though?"

"Hong Kong?" Nicole said. "That's what the caller ID said."

"How do you know she's still even in Hong Kong?" Nathan said. "She could be anywhere in the world and still have a Hong Kong number."

"Where else would she be?" Nicole asked. "That's where she was sent, and I don't think she had the funds or resources to relocate, let alone a plane ticket."

Nicole thought for a moment, imagining her mother's frame of mind at a time like this. This didn't feel planned; as though her mother decided on a spur of a moment to drop everything and leave. Perhaps, overcome by emotions and impatience, Chyanne decided to throw caution to the wind and take to the skies in her dragon form. If so, how on earth was she going to do it? She'd have to stop somewhere, in other countries, like steppingstones across a pond. Then, she'd have to navigate the lower forty-eight.

Whatever the situation, it seemed like a recipe for disaster.

"Did you try calling her back?" Nathan asked.

"I did, but I couldn't leave a message," Nicole responded.

"There's got to be someone we can talk to," Nathan said. "To figure out a way we can pinpoint her location, maybe try to help her find us if she gets lost–"

"I got it," Nicole said. She grabbed her phone and forwarded the message to her uncle with a text asking him to call her as soon as possible. The message was sent, and Nicole put the phone down again.

"Uncle Ishkode is staying at one of my dad's former properties near Central Park," Nicole said, "along with Seth and Joel. They're staying there to assist in the recovery efforts and were going to meet at the UN assembly with the G7. Ishkode will be here for a few weeks while the dust settles." She looked back at her phone. "I don't expect we'll be hearing from him until later. He's probably still asleep."

"Well, what can we do to kill time?" Nathan asked.

Nicole put her arm around him and kissed him on the cheek.

CHAPTER 2

Hours later, Nicole and Nathan found themselves in the Rose Reading Room at the New York Public Library waiting for Ishkode to meet them. Outside, the drone of traffic lulled Nicole into a daze. She never recovered from her early rise, and there was not enough coffee in the world to wake her. She sat at one of the tables, skimming a newspaper, while Nathan browsed the shelves of reference books that may come in handy once he went to school. She wondered how he would do in college as the only weredragon in his freshman class. She hoped he could stand the pressure and avoid the fake friends who wanted to know him simply to say they hung out with a dragon.

"Nicole?" a voice said.

Nicole looked over her shoulder and saw Ishkode standing by the entrance, with Seth to his right. Her uncle looked like a tourist, with a white *I heart NY* shirt, a pair of dark jeans, and a pair of neon-blue sunglasses atop his black, spiky hair. Seth, meanwhile, was still wearing the ragged clothes that he wore when he was living in the tunnels, including a dirty flannel button down and baggy sweatpants that had long since lost their elasticity. Nicole made a mental note to encourage him to buy new clothes once things settled and perhaps get a haircut to tame his graying-blond mane.

She stood up and hugged her uncle, who could have been mistaken for her brother if someone didn't know better. Seth stood by and smiled in his meek sort of way. He wasn't the hugging type, but Nicole knew he had a heart of gold beneath his many layers.

"Thank you for agreeing to meet with us," Nicole said, leading them to their table. She turned to Seth as they sat. "Did you hear the message?"

"I did," he said, gravely. "No doubt it's her. As to how she managed to survive under the radar for so long is anyone's guess."

"But what if it's a deep fake?" Nathan asked, taking a seat. "Some of those are really convincing."

"Yeah, but how did they get a voice sample?" Ishkode said. "Unless someone in Salvini's sphere of influence recorded her a decade ago, I doubt there would be any way for them to reproduce her voice."

"True," Nathan said.

"Still," Nicole said, "why now? Why did she leave me to sit around and think she was dead all these years?"

"To hide from your father," Seth said.

"But why couldn't she take me to wherever she was?" Nicole said.

"Perhaps she had no choice," Ishkode said. "I've been thinking about it, and perhaps she was held against her will."

The thought had indeed gone through Nicole's mind at least once over the last few hours, but at the same time it didn't make a lot of sense. If she was being held, why would they release her now? This had to be her doing

"But regardless, how is she going to get here?" Nicole said. "If she were flying using her wings, how would she do it?"

"Well," Seth said, "we've been talking about that ourselves." He motioned to Ishkode, who took out a folded piece of paper from his back pocket. He unfolded it to reveal a map of Asia. A red line had been drawn from Hong Kong through Taiwan and into Japan, after which it branched off in different directions towards the United States.

Ishkode took out a red marker and pointed it at the line

touching Taiwan. "She would probably head here first, then make her way north towards Japan, stopping somewhere in or near Okinawa." He circled a small speck of land on the map halfway between Taiwan and Japan's largest island. "From there, she'd likely head to the mainland, then fly to Hawaii. After that, it's anyone's guess. She could continue east, towards California, or north towards Alaska. There are some small islands scattered in between, but it's going to be a long trip, and a dangerous one at that."

"It's happened before," Seth said. "Before planes were invented, weredragons who didn't want to sail flew over the oceans. It was actually faster than sailing, though arguably more treacherous. Most weredragons flew in groups, but I've heard of a few who've flown alone."

"But that's not the end of it," Ishkode said. "Not sure how up–to-date you are on the news, but there's a typhoon slamming into southern Japan right now, and no, I'm not talking about your little friend from before." He winked at Nathan, who gave little in the way of a response. Nicole figured his experience with the evil Elder Dragon named Typhoon was still too raw in his mind for him to start cracking jokes about it.

Ishkode took the newspaper Nicole had been reading earlier and flipped through the pages, until he found an article titled *Monsoons Batter Asia, Bringing Record-Setting Rain, Flooding*. Nicole skimmed the body, read of the canceled flights and mudslides, the search and rescue efforts and the blackouts, and grew anxious. Was this what her mother was flying into? And if something went wrong, who would save her?

"If she's smart," Seth said, "she'll stop somewhere and wait it out. But if not, she could become lost and spend an inordinate amount of time flying in circles within the eye of the storm until her wings give out. I don't mean to sound cold, but this is a difficult situation we've got here."

Nicole felt Nathan's hand on her shoulder, felt him rub her back in an effort to calm her. She looked down at the newspaper, at the photo of a semi-truck submerged in brown water, and felt a cold feeling creep through her. Somewhere, her mother was in a battle against the elements, and there was nothing she could do to help her.

CHAPTER 3

Chyanne made good progress initially. Propelled by nothing but her wings and her willpower, she skipped over Taiwan and plotted her path towards Japan. She felt not the sting of hunger pains, nor the craving for a cigarette, or even the want for a drink. Her desire to see Nicole compelled her forward, until the first drops of rain began to fall. Soon, sheets of rain soaked her white and blue scales, while wind pressed against her wings and the skies darkened around her. She felt she was swimming in the sky, immersed by thick, black clouds that were occasionally lit by lightning. Chyanne pressed forward, determined to make it to Tokyo by midnight, but the storm caused the hours of flying to catch up with her, and she grew fatigued.

By nightfall, Chyanne gave up and descended towards the nearest cluster of lights. She landed along a pebbly beach and turned into her human form and was reminded of how poorly she thought this journey though. She hadn't brought any clothes except what she was wearing when she left: a tank top, sweatpants, and a pair of foam flip-flops, like one would wear during a pedicure. She was soaked to her skin, a few bank notes, her cellphone—but not its charger—a lighter, and a pack of cigarettes that were probably waterlogged. She walked up the beach, her arms pressed against her, and braced herself as the rain fell harder. Judging by the concrete buildings and kanji script written in peeling, salt-warn paint, she assumed she was in Okinawa. She emerged onto an empty street, lined with dark houses, lit only with dim streetlamps that swayed in the strong wind rolling off the shore. The waves behind her crashed and tumbled onto the beach, mulling with the rain to create a salty concoction that tasted like tears on her lips. The water coiled around storm drains, tumbled out of gutters, splattered off the pavement and steamed in the balmy nighttime air. Chyanne felt crushed beneath the downpour and more alone than in all her eighty years on this earth. As she walked down the dark sidewalk, looking for a garage port or an awning to sleep under, she clutched herself tighter, and felt the scars on her arms. Little crisscrossed scars, memories of a time long past, nightmares of lonesomeness she wished never to repeat.

As Chyanne looked for any place she could lay her head for the night, she noticed a kei truck pull through the intersection ahead of her and into a street to her left. Curious, she followed and found an open Izakaya, or a bar, its front lit with rice paper lanterns that danced in the frantic breeze. Chyanne entered the small establishment and was greeted by a friendly warmth that was accompanied by a savory smell from the kitchen, mixed with the aroma of Japanese cedar from the wooden walls and tables. The place was empty except for a cluster of rough-looking fishermen, who chatted amongst themselves at a table near the bar. Their conversation stalled as Chyanne's flip flops made squishy sounds off the dark, glossy floor. She pulled up a stool and was greeted by the bartender, a middle-aged man with baggy eyes and a friendly aura.

Chyanne pulled out a soaked one-hundred Hong Kong dollar from her pocket and placed it on the bar. "Sake, hot," she said in fluent Japanese.

The bartender looked down at the note, then her, then back again, his eyes nervous. She could imagine her showing up at his establishment, in this condition and with this currency, was beyond anything he could have imagined, as was her grasp of his language. He nodded and got to work pouring her a hot cup of sake while the fishermen continued their conversation in hushed tones. The bartender handed Chyanne her drink and took the bank note, which he attempted to dry with a nearby rag.

"Keep the change," Chyanne said.

The bartender turned, nodded, and went about fiddling with his cash register while Chyanne took a sip. It was just what she needed, along with a cigarette. She reached into her pocket and took out the pack she had taken with her, hoping the plastic wrapper protected them, but alas, it did not. The pack was soaked through, and she could feel the cigarettes squish and clump together inside. She crushed the pack and tossed it in a nearby waste basket, cursing as she did. She had spent almost seventy-four dollars on that damn pack and only managed to smoke less than half before leaving Hong Kong. Her lighter was probably shot too. She sighed as her cravings began to bite at her.

"Damn you, Lucio," she hissed. He had gotten her hooked on the things, along with hard liquor. She had tried to quit smoking multiple times over the last decade, but each time ended in failure. She cringed at the thought of how much she spent each year on cigarettes, in a country with some of the highest tobacco prices on earth. She could have easily bought a used Civic with the amount of money that literally went up in smoke. Alcohol wasn't a concern for her, though; she had been a heavy drinker before she met Lucio. The only thing that changed was her taste. She went from kicking back Molsons to sipping cognac and other such spirits. She drank most every day, often before bed, and sometimes in the morning with her coffee. She couldn't remember the last time she woke up without some variety of a hangover, and made it a point to keep a bottle of Alka-Seltzer by her nightstand. The longest she had gone without drinking was when she was pregnant with Nicole, which was easily the hardest nine months of her life. But that, of course, was before her drinking became as habitual as it is today.

In the end though, it didn't matter. Dragonets could be harmed by alcohol in the womb, but adults were different. She knew she would never die from cancer or cirrhosis, a benefit of being a weredragon of sorts, though it also meant there was one less exit strategy if life became too unbearable. She felt her scars again, like a roadmap of pain on her arms.

The door at the rear of the establishment opened, and the squeak of wet rubber soles against the slick floor made their way up to the bar. A man pulled up a barstool and sat to Chyanne's left. He was Japanese with slick, short hair that was combed to his left. He had a clean-shaven face and thin spectacles like those of an accountant. He wore a typical salaryman business suit, black with a black tie, and a tan rain jacket hung over his shoulders. The bartender came up to the man to take his order.

"Dom Perigon?" the man asked.

"Is 2013 okay?" the bartender responded.

"I prefer the 2012, but 2013 will do," the man replied.

The bartender poured the drink and handed the man his glass, which he took and held up to his nose, inhaling the aroma. "You're a long way from home, Miss Newheart," he said in English.

Chyanne turned to the man with a cold look. "How the hell do you know my name?" she responded.

"Your handlers in Hong Kong called us," the man replied. "They asked the Tokyo Sanctum for help in locating you. They said they saw you flying east, and when the Taipei Sanctum came back with no answer, they called us." He took a sip of his drink and glanced at Chyanne. "They're worried you're having a mental health crisis."

"Well, they can cool it," she said. "I'm perfectly capable of my own faculties."

"And you left Hong Kong for what, may I ask?"

"None of your business," Chyanne snapped. "Who the hell are you anyway, and how did you know where to find me?"

The man put down his glass and extended a hand. "My name is Daisuke Ikeda. I am the leader of the Hiroshima Satellite of the Tokyo Sanctum. Your handlers told me that you would probably be in a bar, and seeing as this is the only bar open in Okinawa during this typhoon, I assumed you would stop here first."

Chyanne ignored his open palm and turned back to her drink. "They don't know me. To hell with them anyway. All they thought I could do was stitch suits and scrub tile. They never thought I could fly this way by myself."

"Is it because of your daughter?" Daisuke asked. "She's been in the press a lot lately, due to her misadventures in New York."

"I told you, it's none of your damn business," Chyanne said. "And if you think you can drag me back off to Hong Kong, forget it. I'll fight you for it."

The patrons and the bartender glanced at Chyanne nervously, as she realized her outburst was louder than she intended.

"I'm not here for that," Daisuke said. "I'm here for something else."

Chyanne said nothing.

"Have you ever heard of the Yamata no Orochi?"

"Ancient Japanese legend about an eight headed dragon," Chyanne said. "Been there, done that, bought the t-shirt."

"It's more than a legend, though," Daisuke said, lowering his voice. "It's real, and most of all, its legacy lives on."

"What are you trying to pull?" Chyanne said. "Do you take me for a fool?"

"No," Daisuke said. "But you should know by now that the world of weredragons is never as it seems. Before the Orochi was slain by the god of the sea, Susanoo, it laid an egg beneath the mountain known as Sentsu in Okuizumo and Shimane Prefectures. That egg has not been seen in almost two-thousand years, and many weredragons have lusted after it so they may imprint upon its hatchling and control it for their own purposes." He took another sip. "Most recently, your ex, Lucio Salvini."

"What a hair-brained idea," Chyanne said. "Sounds just like him, too, to do something like that. What, did he want to use it to help him take over the world?"

"In a way," Daisuke said. "Before World War II, the

weredragons of Japan were independent, but after the bombs were dropped, Lucio leveraged the allies' victory as a way to force us to join the Confederacy of Sanctums. He then made us search for the missing egg, so that he could include Orochi in the Scales of Rage. But we did not do so willingly, and worked behind his back sabotaging the efforts, delaying the search indefinitely."

"I can't believe I dated that man," Chyanne said, finishing her sake. "Nicole was the only good thing that ever came out of that relationship."

"Now that he's dead," Daisuke continued, "the Tokyo Sanctum and its affiliated satellites have all declared independence, but the egg of the Orochi is beginning to toil. Seismic activity around the mountain is believed to be the egg trying to uncover itself in preparation for its eventual hatching, and if it imprints upon the wrong dragon, it could be the end of the world as we know it. And we have reason to believe that the Elder Typhoon has taken a keen interest in the egg as well."

Chyanne turned to Daisuke. "My ex's babysitter? That old creep?"

Daisuke nodded.

"So what, you want the Orochi's rugrat to imprint on me?" Chyanne asked. "I don't know if you've noticed by now, but my World's Best Mom award hasn't arrived just yet."

"No, but your daughter might be a good applicant," Daisuke said.

"Why her?"

"Why not?" Daisuke said. "She helped bring down Lucio, ended centuries of strife and conflict, and she's the Millennium Hatchling, giving her the most blessed birthdate of anyone in dragonkind."

Chyanne sighed and rubbed her eyes. "First of all, I don't know if you remember or not, but it was her boyfriend, Nathan, who killed Lucio. I saw the video on YouTube. Yeah, she helped, but Nathan was the one who stabbed him in the neck, not her. Second, why is everyone so obsessed with her birthdate? Yes, she may be the first weredragon born in the twenty-first century.

I should know, I was there. But ever since I gave birth to her, everyone around me goes on and on about how important this makes her. She's more than a goddamn date, you know. She's a woman with her own wants and needs, and she doesn't deserve to be someone's puppet."

"But think of the implications," Daisuke said. "If Nicole allows the Orochi to imprint on her, she could tame it. She could even tell it to serve us, and it would listen to her. She could divert Armageddon, but only if she comes to Japan first."

"Why can't you just get someone from your sanctum to do it for you?"

Daisuke finished his drink and set the glass down. "Some of our more *sensitive* members have indicated that Nicole's involvement with your ex brought her to the Orochi's attention, and now it wants her to tame it."

He turned on the barstool to face Chyanne, and she noticed his eyes changed to a shade of bright green.

"Many of the members of the Hiroshima Satellite possess an extra sense. A third eye if you will. I have it too, and I know that your daughter will be the best candidate for taming the Orochi."

* * *

Before Chyanne could respond, Daisuke's expression darkened, and he lunged forward. He knocked Chyanne off her stool, sending her sake glass tumbling. Chyanne was about to shove him off, when the front window exploded and the glasses behind the bar began to pop and shatter. The bartender screamed and ducked, while the patrons got under their table. All the while, a cracking sound, like that of a firecracker, rattled off the walls and ceiling in rapid succession. It was the unmistakable sound of a machine pistol, firing at full auto. The shooting stopped, and Chyanne turned to see a silver car speed away, its rear wheels skidding on the wet pavement.

Chyanne sprang to her feet and ran to the entrance, leaping over the shattered window and into the rain-slick street, and saw the car's taillights peel off into the distance. Chyanne transformed into her dragon form and flew as fast as she could to keep up with it, fighting the wind and rain as she did. Even with such poor visibility, she could tell it was an old Honda NSX, with pop up headlights and a slender profile. Chyanne felt her fire climb up her throat, ready to let loose a jet of flames and reduce the car to ash.

Before she could torch it, something large collided with her, sending her hurtling through the air and into a nearby structure. Chyanne's skull met concrete and crashed through a thick wall. She clawed her way to her feet, her legs nearly giving out on her as she struggled to maintain balance against the waves of dizziness that overcame her. She felt a pair of talons wrap around her neck and force her down, pressing her against the pavement. A large dragon stood over her, its yellow eyes piercing hers with a venomous look.

"You should've stayed in Hong Kong, Chy," her attacker said with a heavy Eastern-European accent. He pressed down on Chyanne's neck, nearly crushing her windpipe beneath him. Chyanne struggled for air and tried to pry the dragon's meaty claws off of her, but he was too strong. Seconds from passing out, she felt something cool and metallic press against her thigh. She reached down, and found it was a piece of rebar that was loosened when she crashed through the wall. She grabbed it and, thinking only on impulse, jammed the rebar into the dragon's groin.

The dragon screamed and let her go, allowing her to roll out of the way and spring to her feet. Before the dragon could react, she whirled around and smacked him with her tail, sending him tumbling into what remained of the building. With the rebar still in hand, she sprang upon her attacker and bent the steel back and around his neck like a garrote. She twisted the steel into a knot and pulled up, so that it dug into his scales and cut into his airways. The dragon balanced on his toes, clawed at the rebar, but Chyanne only pulled harder. She loosened her grasp just enough to let him speak.

"Who sent you?" she asked.

"I work alone," the dragon said.

"Liar!" Chyanne said. "Guns are impossible to come by in Japan, so you have to be working with someone with a lot of connections. Who is it?" She tightened her grasp.

"Typhoon," the dragon gasped. "He wants you to help him with the Orochi."

"You mean he wants my daughter to help him?" Chyanne said. "Well guess what, buddy, she's not going to play along with your little game. I'll die before I let him get a hold of her."

"It's more complicated than that," the dragon said. "Tauri–"

There was a crack, and the dragon's head slumped down. Chyanne felt blood against her talons and looked to find the dragon's right eyeball was gone, replaced by a fleshy hole that bled like a geyser. An exit wound on the opposite side of the head confirmed that someone had shot the dragon through the eye with a high-powered rifle.

A car door slammed, and Chyanne looked up to see the same NSX from earlier speeding off into the distance, its exhaust rattling into the night. Chyanne let go of the dragon's corpse and stepped back. Who was Tauri? She thought she heard the name before, but couldn't tell when or where, and she had no idea how he was in conjunction with everything else.

A second dragon, this one a wingless serpentine with jade scales, a blue mane, and matching whiskers landed across from Chyanne. "Are you okay?" the dragon asked. It was Daisuke.

"I am," she said. "It was a setup by Typhoon to try and capture me. He's got the same idea as you and your crew and wants to use my daughter to crack the egg and let the Orochi imprint on her."

"Why would he want to do that?"

"I don't know," Chyanne said. "But he's after Nicole, and that's all I care about. And you are going to help me keep her safe." She wiped the blood off her scales. "You want her to help you so badly, fine, but you're paying for her plane ticket, and if she gets too knee deep in the hoopla the deal is off. Understand?"

"I'll do everything in my power," Daisuke said. "But we have to get out of here before the authorities show up."

Sure enough, Chyanne heard the distant whine of a police cruiser coming towards them.

"Follow me," Daisuke said, launching himself into the air. "If we fly now, we can make it to the mainland by this time tomorrow. We can book a train from Kagoshima to Hiroshima, and you can try contacting Nicole along the way."

"Weather permitting," Chyanne said, following Daisuke. "Though I think the rain is starting to lighten up."

The rain was beginning to ease, though the drops still pelted her as she followed Daisuke over the dark ocean waves.

"Quick question," she said. "How can you fly without wings?" She had just noticed that Daisuke seemingly bent and swerved through the air like an eel, despite not having any wings to show for. He was sort of like the weredragons she had seen in Hong Kong, many of whom were of the same type: long, snake-like, with a frill down their back. But no wings.

"I don't really know," Daisuke said. "To me, flying feels like swimming, so leaping into the air is like jumping into a body of water. It's hard to explain unless you're a serpentine dragon like myself. I'm sure other dragons have different ways of describing it."

"Fair enough," Chyanne said as they pressed forward.

CHAPTER 4

A day after their meeting in the library, Nicole found herself in Nathan's living room, sitting in front of a large box bearing the initials FBI. Someone from the New York field office had dropped it off earlier that day, with a letter:

Dear Ms. Newheart,

On July 12th, 2022, the Federal Bureau of Investigation executed a search warrant for your father's estate in Montauk. During the search, our agents discovered a number of effects that pertain to your late mother, Chyanne Newheart. As you are her only known last of kin, and because these items do not hold any intrinsic value to our investigation into the whereabouts of your brother, Lucca Salvini, we have relinquished these items to you. Please notify our field office right away if you have any questions or if you feel there is a mistake with the items we have collected.

The letter was signed with the name of the agent who had led the raid, along with their badge number. Nicole sat there, reading the letter again and staring at the box as though she expected it to come to life and speak to her. Part of her was afraid to look inside, worried about what she might find. She was tempted to place the box in the nearest closet and never open it, but she knew if she did that, she would spend the rest of her life ruminating on its contents.

"Well," Nathan asked. "Are you going to open it?"

Nicole ran her fingers along the side of the lid. She felt bad her uncle couldn't be here, but he had to fly back to Canada at the last minute. He was meeting with members of the Quebec Sanctum, with the hopes of locating her mother and bringing her back to North America in one piece. He told Nicole to snap pictures of the contents and send them to him as soon as she was able.

"It feels like ripping off a bandage," Nicole said. "And I don't know if it's healed yet."

Nathan put his hand on her shoulders, working his way to the spot where her neck ended and her back began, and rubbed the spot where her tension tended to settle. She leaned into his touch, letting him work the strain out from under her muscles. She gripped the side of the lid, and ripped off the masking tape.

The box was full of random objects that typical people acquired in a lifetime. She took out an expired Quebec driver's license and an old provincial health insurance card. Both showed a photo of Chyanne from when Nicole remembered her most, with long black locks, and a smile on her off-tan face. There was a small Atkanw nation flag, about the size of a handkerchief, along with a cigarette lighter with the Fleur-de-lis engraved on it. Nicole shook the lighter to check for fuel, and found there was still some inside. She knew her mom smoked, and while she had always found it a dirty practice, she had long accepted it as part of who she was.

"What's that?" Nathan asked. He was pointing to a blue pin at the bottom of the box with the words *Oui* written in bold white lettering.

Nicole grabbed it. "It's a *Leave* button," she said. "From the time Quebec tried to vote to leave Canada in 1980." She put the button down and picked up another object, a small flask, wrapped in brown leather with a maple leaf engraved on it, yet another reminder of her mother's vices.

The final object in the box was a worn, hardcover copy of *Oryx and Crake* by Margot Atwood. The cover showed a dried, crusty landscape, deprived of water, with the shadow of a man cast over it, his arm bent as though he was protecting his eyes from the sun. It seemed well read, with its dustjacket torn in some places and the edges of its pages yellowed. As she observed the book, she noticed a piece of paper sticking out from between the pages. She pulled it out, and made eye contact with the face of her mother from the last time she had seen her.

The picture showed Chyanne Newheart, standing at the bottom of a flight of stairs that was leading to the entrance to a private jet. She pinched a cigarette in her right hand, her other arm folded over her chest. She looked different in this photo from her ID cards: her face was thinner, her hair shorter, her expression emotionless and indifferent. She was wearing a white hoodie and a pair of sweatpants with a visible tear along her left knee, and a pair of dirtied sneakers. Her skin was oily, and there were dark circles under her eyes. She looked at the camera with a blank expression, as though whoever took the photo had caught her off guard. There was something sad behind her expression, something Nicole felt only she could notice, like an invisible message passed between mother and daughter. It was an expression Nicole learned to read before her mother was sent away, one that Chyanne tried so desperately to hide behind a mask of contentment, but which Nicole always managed to see with clarity.

It was a look of dread.

The date at the bottom of the picture confirmed this suspicion: January 11, 2013.

"I think this was taken the day she was sent to Hong Kong," Nicole said.

She stared at the photo for what felt like hours, studying its every feature. She recalled her mother's appearance before she was left in the New York Sanctum. The worry and the fear of her father ate away at her, leaving her a hollowed husk of the person she used to be. She wished she could reach through the photo, through the annals of time, and tell her mother it was all going to be okay, and that everything would work out in the end. She placed the photo back in the book and scanned the other items that lay before her. Figments of a life that had been kept and preserved for reasons she did not understand, with questions she could not begin to fathom.

Nicole's phone began to ring. She froze; could it be? She pulled herself up and went to the kitchen, where her phone was charging next to the coffee maker.

The caller ID was clear as day: *Unknown Number Hong Kong SAR.*

Nicole took a sharp breath as she unplugged the phone and placed her thumb over the green answer icon. "It's her," she said.

CHAPTER 5

A bath, a good meal, and eight hours of sleep did Chyanne good. After having spent so much time flying over endless oceans and battling all that mother nature could throw at her, she was relieved to be somewhere with a roof over her head. She was in Hiroshima, in an apartment owned by Daisuke, having been given time to recuperate after her encounter in Okinawa. Daisuke had already introduced her to several of his colleagues and laid out the plan of action for what was next. Once they established contact with Nicole, and paid for her flight, Daisuke would drive them to Mt. Sentsu and begin searching for the egg.

That was the easy part. The hard part, at least for Chyanne, was contacting her daughter.

Chyanne looked out over Hiroshima's harbor, the still water dotted with ships that traversed its dark, glassy surface. It was long past evening, close to midnight, and the city was winding down for the night. The hum of traffic and the whine of bullet trains had died down, and Chyanne felt herself at peace for the first time in days. This was not like Hong Kong, which was always loud and congested at all hours of the day or night. Here, she felt she could get a good night's rest without worrying about the old lift waking her up or having to break up a row between her neighbors in their stuffy high-rise. She reclined on the chair that sat atop the balcony overlooking the city, felt the cool night air run up her arms and legs. She wore a kimono that she found in the closet, its black fabric spotted with flowers of red and yellow. She didn't know if kimonos were gendered, or if she was even wearing it correctly, but it was comfortable nonetheless.

She picked up her phone and flipped it open. It had, in spite of the rain, survived the journey, and still managed to hold a charge, a testament to archaic cellphone design that modern smartphones seemingly lacked. She maneuvered to her 'recent' folder and selected Nicole's number, then, after staring at the number for what felt like forever, pressed the button labeled *OK*. She put the phone up to her ear, and waited.

It rang once, twice, three times. Maybe Nicole was out and unable to answer. Maybe she could try again tomorrow when it was easier for the both of them. Or maybe Nicole had blocked her and wanted nothing to do with her. In that case, she could take the matter off of her hands and let it be someone else's problem. But no, that couldn't be the case. Why would Nicole ignore her?

The tone rang again.

Of course, who would want to talk to a mother who abandoned them and left them for dead? Who let her think that she had died so that she wouldn't try to contact her? Chyanne knew that if she was in such a situation, she'd curse her mother with every word she knew.

The tone rang again.

Chyanne ran her nails up and down her arms, scratching the scars she had made years ago, back when it felt like all hope was lost and that her life was forever at the mercy of others. She had originally done it to alleviate her nerves, but soon she started to cut down, lengthwise. *Sideways for attention, longways for results.*

The tone rang again.

Her heart raced. Her hands shook. Her mouth became dry. And she felt the walls of the apartment closing in on her. She bit her lip, dug her nails into the wood of the chair. She started imagining what her daughter would say if they were face-to-face. Nicole would probably smack her, shout and scream, and it would all be deserved. Chyanne nearly chucked the phone off the balcony . . .

"Hello?"

Chyanne froze. It was Nicole's voice, her tone, exactly as she had sounded on her voicemail greeting. She felt the world give out from under her, and in an instant, she was light as a feather.

"Nicole?" Chyanne asked.

"Mom?" Nicole said. Her voice was shaky, like she was on the verge of tears.

"Yes," Chyanne said, through tears of her own. "I missed you so much."

The two burst into tears and exchanged words of joy and jubilation.

"How have you been, baby girl?" Chyanne asked.

"I've been okay," Nicole responded. *"Seth and Joel raised me well, and I've got a boyfriend now."*

"I've heard. How has he been treating you?"

"I love him, Mom," Nicole said. *"He's great, Nathan."*

"The fact that he killed your father makes him a keeper in my book," Chyanne said with a slight laugh. "Baby girl, I'm so sorry for abandoning you."

"You didn't abandon me," Nicole said. *"You left me with great people, and you did everything you could to protect me."*

"Oh child," Chyanne said. "I did it out of desperation. I was powerless to save you from your father's intentions, so I did the only thing I thought I could. And when he shipped me off to Hong Kong, I . . ."

"What is it?"

Chyanne sighed, her voice wavering. "Baby, you were under the impression that I took my life. The truth is that I wanted to, and I tried, several times. I wanted to die so badly, I didn't want to live in a world where I couldn't see you again, and I blamed myself for putting you in such a situation."

"Mom, I'm so sorry."

"But someone came to save me," Chyanne said. "Some benevolent members of the Hong Kong Sanctum healed me, hid me away from Lucio's cronies, gave me a roof over my head and job training. I worked at a bespoke tailor, until it went bankrupt. I had a life of my own there. But they forbid me to contact you, for your safety, and my own, until your father's death."

"*Where are you now?*" Nicole asked.

"I'm in Hiroshima," Chyanne said. "Nicole, I have a strange request of you."

"*What is it?*"

Chyanne told her all about her misadventures in Okinawa, including her involvement with Daisuke Ikeda, the Hiroshima Satellite, and where Nicole fitted into the legend of the Yamata no Orochi. When Chyanne finished, she paused and waited for a response.

"*So, you want me to come to Japan?*" Nicole asked.

"I understand if you don't want to," Chyanne said. "And the Tokyo Sanctum has backups for the Orochi to imprint on. They really just want you to tell it to obey them no matter what, and then you'll be done and can go back, but–"

"*I'll do it,*" Nicole said.

"You . . . you will?"

"*I can get on the next flight if possible.*"

"Really?" Chyanne said. "You don't have to rush, you know. Personally, between you and me, I think the Tokyo Sanctum is taking the immediacy of the situation too far."

"*It's fine,*" Nicole said. "*I just want to see you again.*"

Chyanne exhaled and felt her body decompress. This was easier than she thought.

"Is Nathan there?" she asked.

"*Yes,*" Nicole said. "*He's been listening in on the speaker this whole time.*"

"May I speak to him please?" Chyanne said. "Without the speaker?"

"*Um, sure,*" Nicole said. "*Hold on real quick.*"

There was the sound of the phone being passed around,

followed by the rubbing of someone's ear against the receiver.

"Hello, Ms. Newheart?" Nathan's voice asked. He sounded young, as though his voice still hadn't shed the last of his fleeting adolescence.

"Call my Chyanne, or Chy," Chyanne said. "I don't do surnames."

"Okay, Chyanne," Nathan said.

"That's better," Chyanne said. *"Now tell me, Nate, did Lucio say anything before you killed him?"*

"Um, he begged Nicole for his life," Nathan said. *"After that it was just a guttural scream as he plummeted from the Empire State Building. Why do you ask?"*

Chyanne closed her eyes and tried to imagine the pain he went through, the joyous moment when all his roosters came to roost and his sins came back to bite him in the ass.

"I just wanted to know," Chyanne said. "Now listen, Nate, and listen very carefully. As you can imagine, I have a natural distrust of certain men, and I don't know you well enough to say I trust you with my daughter. Ikeda- San is just a means to an end for all I care. As for you, if you do anything to hurt my daughter, or do anything to break her heart, I will hurt you. Killing Lucio put you high on my list, but Nicole is the only person in this world that I care about, and she's the only reason why I haven't attempted suicide in over a decade. If you do so much as make her cry, I'll make it so you'll have to legally change your name to Nathania by the time I'm done with you. Understand?"

"Ye--yes," Nathan said.

"Good," Chyanne said. "Put Nicole back on the phone."

There was a pause, and a flurry of voices, before Nicole came back on.

"Mom, what did you say to Nathan?" she asked. *"He's turned pale."*

"Oh, nothing dear," Chyanne said. "Now, I don't suppose you know anyone by the name of Tauri, do you?"

"Like Tauri Allerton?" Nicole said. *"That's Seth's son with his late wife. Why?"*

Chyanne felt a rush of chills down her back, and her arms and legs rippled into gooseflesh. She had forgotten all about the eldest Allerton boy, the only surviving descendant and the one who joined Lucio centuries ago.

"The dragon who attacked me in Okinawa said his name before he died," Chyanne said. "I didn't know who he meant at the time, but now I wonder."

"I'll have to run it by Seth first," Nicole said. *"He may want to talk with you about it."*

"Yeah," Chyanne said, absentmindedly. "Maybe he can clear the air."

There was a brief pause, after which Chyanne yawned, the weight of the night bearing down on her like the rain from earlier.

"Well, baby girl, I'm going to go to bed," she said. "It's past midnight here. Tomorrow, I'll tell Ikeda-San all about our chat and see if he can book you the next flight to Hiroshima."

"Okay, Mom," Nicole said. *"Sleep well."*

"Thanks honey," she said. "I'll try."

"I love you," Nicole said. *"It was nice talking to you."*

"I love you too," Chyanne replied. "Goodbye."

"Goodnight."

Chyanne closed her phone and looked out over the harbor. I love you. Three words that took so little room on a page but said so much. Chyanne placed her phone on the arm of her chair and looked up at the stars, thinking of her baby, now a woman, with a life and goals of her own. She closed her eyes and as she slipped off to sleep, and prayed to whoever was listening that Nicole would grow strong and safe, and that Nathan would love and protect her.

CHAPTER 6

Twenty-four hours later, Nicole and Seth were on a plane to Los Angeles, whereupon they would take a connection to Hawaii to Hiroshima. Upon learning that Tauri might be involved, Seth arranged with the Hiroshima Sanctum to let him come along for support, though Nicole could already tell he had his own plans in mind. Nathan was not with them. Following a brief conversation after the phone call was over, the two came to an agreement that he should not come. This was a Newheart matter, one that Nathan was not privy enough to get involved in, and he agreed it was best for him to stay behind. And so, on the day she left, Nicole and Nathan said a long, agonizing goodbye in the main terminal of JFK, like the end of a sappy romcom. Then he was gone, and Nicole was separated from him for the first time since the battle in DC. As she boarded the flight and braced herself for the plane's takeoff, a heaviness hung in her heart along with a sense of loneliness she hadn't felt since before their relationship began. She had no idea how long they would be apart, unable to talk except on the phone and when the time zones permitted. She didn't think it would be this hard, but as the skies drifted past her window, the reality of her situation set in, and a longing for Nathan burrowed deep inside her.

To try to take her mind off it, she kept herself occupied by reading *Oryx and Crake*. Nicole was ashamed to admit she wasn't the best reader; the dim tunnels were not particularly conducive for reading, and despite Seth's best efforts to get her an education, she dropped out of school at sixteen once it was no longer a viable option. As such, she often avoided reading for pleasure because she worried it would make her feel stupid. These feelings came back after she started reading the novel and struggled through the first few chapters, until it dawned on her that the story was told in a non-linear style. Eventually, as the hours ticked by, and the plane moved from connection to connection, and as Seth drifted in and out of a Dramamine-induced coma, Nicole found herself hooked. Between cat naps, she would read as much as she could, and she managed to finish the book a few hours after they left Hawaii. The adventures of Snowman and the mutant abominations born of human greed left Nicole feeling fulfilled, and she fell asleep with dreams of one day going back to school, earning her GED, and possibly more.

The plane landed in Hiroshima Airport around lunchtime, some thirty-six hours after leaving New York. Upon docking at the terminal, Nicole nudged Seth awake, then called Daisuke, to inform them the eagle had landed. Daisuke gave them his location, and then they left to go to customs, before heading to baggage.

"Do I look like a tourist?" Seth asked through a yawn as they walked towards the conveyor belt.

"Is the sky blue?" Nicole asked. "Relax, I'm sure I have you beat." Her jean jacket, with the Canadian maple leaf on the back and provincial flags of Quebec and Nova Scotia on the shoulders, was a dead giveaway. She wondered how her mom would react to the sight of the Atkanw Nation flag she had added long after she went into hiding. Seth was a bit more discreet, with a black V-neck and a pair of tan cargo pants, but he was still a dirty-blond Caucasian man in the middle of Japan. At least he had gotten a haircut and a shave before he left, leaving him a little less scruffy than he was before.

"You ever been to Japan before?" Nicole asked.

He nodded. "Over a century ago," he said. "I came to Tokyo

to discuss sanctum relationships in response to the Russo-Japanese War of 1904."

"Sounds thrilling," Nicole said.

"It was a waste of time," he said. "I sat and listened while weredragons from Vladivostok and Manchuria argued for an hour and then everyone left without any progress. The Confederacy of Sanctums swallowed them up forty years later."

Nicole nodded along. She was going to say something about the sanctums being liberated, and the Confederacy no longer posing a threat, but without Joel here to counter him, she would be rebuked by Seth's brand of lukewarm cynicism. Seth would never be satisfied with the state of things, given all that he had seen in his almost five-hundred years of life. She saw it all in the circles under eyes in his human form, which were always dark and set with deep wrinkles. Even the tan scales of his dragon form looked weathered and beaten down, like a piece of old driftwood. He had simply seen too much to not take everything with a heavy grain of salt.

Nicole, someone said, *help me.*

She looked over her shoulder, startled.

"What is it?" Seth asked.

"Did you just call me?"

Seth shook his head.

Nicole shrugged. "Must be jetlag," she said as their baggage came into view.

They grabbed their baggage and made their way down to the main terminal, where Daisuke had said he would meet them. It didn't take long for them to spot the sharply dressed Japanese man holding a sign with their names on it. They approached and shook hands.

"Mr. Ikeda," Nicole said. "It's a pleasure to meet you."

"You too, Ms. Newheart," Daisuke said. "And Mr. Allerton. Welcome to Hiroshima."

"It's changed a lot since I was here last," Seth said. "Though a lot of things have changed since the turn of the last century."

"Well, we're happy that you're here," Daisuke said. "Nicole, your mother is waiting in the car. May I take your luggage?"

They handed their suitcases to Daisuke, and a sudden tense feeling swept over Nicole. She had spoken to her mom over the phone, but now she was going to meet with her in person. How would her mom react to her? How would their first conversation go? They followed Daisuke through departures to a red, boxy-looking vehicle that looked like a minivan had a baby with a shoe box.

"Is that a kei car?" Seth asked.

"It is," Daisuke said. "A Honda N-Box to be more exact. The Tokyo Sanctum and its satellites use them as shuttles."

"They weren't kidding about the box part," Nicole said, observing its bizarre proportions and oddly rectangular height.

No sooner had she started to contemplate what would happen if it was to swerve around a hairpin than Nicole caught a whiff of a cigarette and spotted someone leaning against the car's rear. The cigarette fell and the figure crushed it beneath a black sneaker. Chyanne emerged from behind the car and froze when she saw Nicole. She was thinner than Nicole remembered, with her cheek bones pressing against the flesh of her pale and sickly face. She wore a black tank top and a pair of black arm sleeves that ended with fingerless gloves. Chyanne stepped forward, her arms crossed, and glanced up at Nicole shyly.

"Hey Mom," Nicole said.

"Hey," Chyanne said.

There was a pause, then Chyanne sprang forward, embraced Nicole, and the waterworks started. Nicole cried until she could cry no longer, the embrace rekindling sweet memories with every beat of their hearts.

Chyanne kissed Nicole on her forehead and ruffled her bangs. "I missed you baby girl," she said.

"I missed you too, Mom," Nicole said. "I brought you something." She reached into the pocket of her jean jacket and handed her mother the Oui pin.

Chyanne laughed when she saw it. "Where did you find that?"

"The FBI found it in Dad's house in Montauk," Nicole said. "I never knew you were a *leave* member."

Chyanne stuck the pin onto the left strap of her tank top and patted it affectionately. "It was something I was into back in the day," she said. "I was always somewhat of a contrarian, even now."

Daisuke came around the hood of the car and patted the bonnet. "We're all packed. Ready to go?"

Chyanne glanced over at Daisuke and nodded. "Yeah, let's hit the road."

* * *

It was a three-hour car ride from Hiroshima's city center to Mt. Sentsu via the E74 Expressway. The drive was mostly uneventful, with stops for gas, food, bathroom and, at least for Chyanne, a smoke break. The conversation in the Honda lingered on the situation at hand: the Orochi, and Typhoon's attempts to gain access to the egg.

"There's been some strange activity by the base of the mountain," Daisuke said, between mouthfuls of Calbee chips. "Recently, a mining company started digging around the base of the mountain, around the same time the seismic activity started. The head honchos back in Tokyo believe it's a shell company, and we've been in contact with the local authorities, but as you can imagine, communication between us and the local police has been hit or miss." He glanced over his shoulder at Nicole. "It wasn't until recently that they found out weredragons exist."

"So, you're saying my father tried to find the egg first," Nicole said. "If that's the case, how did he not manage to find it after all this time?"

"No one really knows where it is," Daisuke said. "It's hidden in the mountain, that's for sure, but where is a mystery. He ordered us years ago to find it, but the going's been slow, thanks to our sabotaging his efforts and the sheer size of the excavation area."

"How are we going to find it then?" Seth asked.

"Ah, you see," Daisuke said. "Ever since the seismic activity began, deep cracks have appeared within the surface of the mountain. Some of our more adventurous types have poked around and it appears to be an inner cave system that may lead to the egg. We suspect we're on the cusp of finding it and letting it imprint on Nicole."

Nicole sat up in her captain's chair. "What exactly do you want me to say to this creature?"

"Tell it to serve us," Daisuke said. "Protect the good-natured dragons of the earth and eat all those who mean us harm."

"Well, that's not morbid at all," Nicole sneered.

"Think again," Daisuke said. "It's not as bad as what would happen if Typhoon got a hold of it."

"What evidence do we have that Typhoon is behind the excavation?" Seth asked.

"Not much, admittedly," Daisuke said. "But the mining company moved in shortly after Lucio's death, and we know that Typhoon has the human connections necessary for such an operation."

"I met Typhoon once," Chyanne said. "He was playing the role of Silvio Contti at a dinner party. Gave off a creepy vibe. He reminded me of a vampire dressed in old mafia attire in a greasy tux that probably hadn't been washed since prohibition. Makes sense that he was the devil all along."

"He tried to tempt Nathan," Nicole said. "During our flight to Maryland, he confronted him at a crossroads while I was asleep."

Chyanne nodded in approval. "He's got bigger balls than I thought," Chyanne said. "It's a shame I couldn't meet him."

"Someday," Nicole said. "Also, what did you say to him on the phone the other day?"

"Just that if he broke your heart there will be hell to pay. Though considering he turned down Satan's golden fiddle, I'd say he's good."

"He seemed nervous after you spoke with him."

Chyanne smiled slyly. "I may have been a little rough on him, but I am your mother." She turned to stare out the window. "Call it overcompensating, but I gotta do what I gotta do."

Daisuke adjusted the rearview mirror and peered into its reflection. "I don't mean to sound alarmist, but I think we're being followed."

Nicole turned to look at the road behind them and saw a silver sports car trailing them on the now deserted highway. The car looked like something from thirty years ago, with sharp edges and pop-up headlights that gave it an oddly retro charm.

"Shit," Chyanne snapped. "That's the same car I saw in Okinawa, the one whose driver shot at us."

"You sure?" Daisuke asked.

"I'm positive," Chyanne said. "It's engraved in my mind."

Nicole observed the car gaining ground, until it was close enough that she could make out a pair of gloved hands gripping the steering wheel.

"I think I know the answer to this," Seth said, "but do you have any chance in hell of outrunning him?"

"In your dreams," Daisuke said. "This thing has less than seventy horsepower. God knows how much he has."

The sports car swerved to the right, pulled ahead in the opposite lane, then suddenly cut them off and slammed on its brakes. Daisuke broke hard to keep from colliding and Nicole' seatbelt locked. When the smoke from the tires cleared, the driver's door opened, and a tall, tanned man stepped out. He had long, black hair, which was tied into a slick ponytail. He wore a goatee that ended in a near-perfect point at the tip of his chin, and his eyes were covered by a pair of round mirror shades. A tan cargo vest covered a camo muscle shirt, upon which a claw dangled from a chain around his neck. The driver approached, his thick army boots clicking off the tarmac, coming to a stop halfway between the two cars.

"Son of a bitch," Seth said. He wrenched his door open and

marched up to their pursuer.

"Hello there, Dad," the driver said. "It's been quite a while since we last spoke."

Seth responded by slapping him across the face. "Don't call me that," he said. "I'm ashamed to be your father."

"*That's* Tauri?" Chyanne asked. "So, he *was* behind my attack in Okinawa."

Nicole took her seat belt off and opened the door.

"Nicole, wait," Chyanne said, but it was too late. Nicole stepped out of the Honda and stopped just short of the hood.

Tauri readjusted his glasses. "Missed you too, Dad. What are you doing here in Japan?"

"Figuring out why your name was on the lips of a dragon with a bullet through his eye. Tell me, Tauri, did you pull that trigger?"

Tauri laughed and patted a small machinegun on his hip. "I was just tying up loose ends, all part of my profession." He reached into a pocket on his vest and held out a business card.

Seth took the card and read it. "Echo Group? Is this a joke?"

"It's a private military," Tauri said, "owned and operated by one Silvio Contti. It's like Wagner, but with more teeth." He glanced at Nicole and nodded. "Hey, Nic. Has anyone ever told you puberty hit you like a bus?"

Eww, Nicole thought.

"So, Typhoon is sending his lackeys to do his dirty work," Seth said. "Your mother and I raised you better than this, to not be the lapdog of a megalomaniac."

"Strong words," Tauri said. "At least I'm contributing something positive, rather than getting involved with human drama." He grasped the claw around his neck and kissed it. "This is Kishil's claw, the only thing I have of him after he died in the skies over Iceland. Everything I do now is for him, to live the life he never had."

"Oh, like your other two brothers?" Seth asked. "Or your own mother? Tell me, Tauri, what went through your head when Skoanon and Pentowit were put to the flame?"

Tauri ruffled his vest and looked down at his father, his eyes boring into him though the top of his sunglasses. "Keep talking, Dad. What I'm doing is bigger than Lucio or the Confederacy. In the end, Lucio knew nothing, but Typhoon has broad plans for us, and you can either join him or stay the hell out of his way."

He made one final nod towards Nicole, before climbing back into his car and speeding off down the highway. Nicole watched him turn round the bend and vanish, while Seth stood there, staring into space, the business card dangling from his fingers.

CHAPTER 7

The remainder of the drive was silent as they pulled into the town of Okuizumo, in the historical province of Izumo. It was nearly evening, and the combination of the ride and jet lag took its toll on Nicole, who was ready to collapse into the nearest bed. They parked next to a flatbed kei truck in the shadow of a large, traditional Japanese-style home that was located near a dirt road leading to the mountains. As Nicole took her suitcase, Daisuke pointed to the largest peak jutting out like the ridges on the back of a large dragon.

"See that," he asked. "That's Mount Sentsu. It's about a two-hour walk, or only twenty minutes by flight."

Nicole stared at the large rock, its peak covered in clouds, and imagined the monster that dwelled within. The mountain felt oddly serene, its features caked in greenery and foliage, betraying the sinister nature of the legend that surrounded it. Nicole could not imagine it being the home to something evil, something that could potentially destroy the world. And yet, she felt a strange pull, a feeling that she needed to be there.

"Is this place yours?" Seth asked.

"Yes, indeed," Daisuke said. "It's belonged to the sanctum for centuries."

Nicole looked at the sprawling estate before her. Its walls were made of darkened wood, while a large, sloping roof was lined with rounded tiles in rows like the bones of a spine.

The house did indeed look old, but comfy, with paper lanterns dangling below the overhanging roof. They were led inside, and Nicole was shown the bedchamber that she would share with her mother. A pair of traditional floor mattresses sat on either side of a rice paper privacy screen, while a sliding door looked out onto a small courtyard adorned with a pond and a footbridge. Nicole took off her jean jacket, revealing a green New York Jets T-shirt she had borrowed from Nathan, and plopped herself down onto the bed closest to the sliding door.

"Better you take the one by the door," Chyanne said as she walked by. "I'd get nervous sleeping by such a large opening. Kind of a superstition that's baked into me." She stepped out into the courtyard and lit a cigarette, far enough away that the smoke wouldn't enter the house, but close enough that she and Nicole could converse. "I don't know what you think of all this," Chyanne said, "but I think we should destroy the egg."

Nicole looked up. "Why?"

"I don't trust this Orochi thing to do as it's told," Chyanne said. "We need to smother it in its crib before it could do us any harm."

"I can see Daisuke's reasoning, though," Nicole said, "considering all the weredragons of Japan have been through."

"Regardless," Chyanne said, flicking away some ash, "this creature is unpredictable, and personally, I'm not sure Ikeda-San knows what he's getting himself into. The road to hell is lined with good intentions, after all."

Nicole rolled onto her stomach and looked out at her mother. "So, what do you suppose we do?"

"Burn the egg," Chyanne said. "Or tell it to off itself. Maybe you can tell it to fly into space and burn itself in the sun. Either way, this thing needs to die, and we can't let the world realize that when it's too late."

Nicole had mixed feelings about the proposition. On the one hand, the world would probably be a better place without the Orochi. But on the other, it seemed like such a waste of scales. If the Free Sanctums had had an Orochi on their side, the battle in New York wouldn't have happened, and Washington DC would not have burned as badly as it did. She could genuinely see some benefits of having a powerful, eight-headed dragon on their side, ready to do their bidding.

I must live.

Nicole looked over her shoulder, but for the second time in a row, the source of the voice was nowhere. Before she could call out to whoever uttered the words, there was a knock at the door. Nicole sprang to her feet and when she slid it open, she saw Seth on the other side. He was holding a freshly opened can of Sapporo, its sliver surface coated with condensation.

"How are you and your mom doing?"

"Fine," Nicole said, stepping aside.

Seth entered, walked to the edge of the courtyard, and sat down on one of the steps.

"How are *you* doing?" Nicole asked, sitting next to him.

Seth shrugged. "I knew I was probably going to meet Tauri at some point during this trip, I just wish it was under different circumstances." He took a sip of his drink. "Part of me wanted to think Tauri would come back to me, now that Lucio is dead. But now, I don't think there's anything I can do to save him."

Chyanne took a drag of her cigarette and exhaled. "He had the same Ingram he used to shoot at me and Daisuke in Okinawa."

"He was gloating," Seth said. "I don't know where he got it from, but it was something I never could wean out of him."

Chyanne flicked some more ash onto the gravel, its scarlet hue rabidly changing to grey as the air cooled it. "My curiosity is killing me," she said, "but if there's an open wound in this story, please don't rip the bandage off for me."

"Bah," Seth said. "I've told this story before. Tauri is my eldest child. Atabey, my wife, was killed by Lucio, along with my two youngest, after I refused to give her over to him. Lucio convinced Tauri and his younger brother, Kishil, to join him. Kishil, as you can probably guess, is dead, so Tauri is my only living child." Seth paused. "Father's Day in the Allerton household is complicated."

Nicole observed Seth's stony expression change slightly, his eyes moistening like they were preparing to weep in spite of his feigned indifference. She touched Seth's arm, and he glanced at her with a sorrowful expression.

"Jesus," Chyanne said, stamping out her cigarette. "I knew you had a rough past, but I had no idea about your family."

Seth put his arm around Nicole's shoulder and pulled her close. "It's fine because Nicole was like the daughter I never had, and she turned out better than Tauri could ever hope to be."

"All thanks to you," Chyanne said. "I knew you were a good man the moment Lucio started cursing your name. Every enemy of Lucio is a good person as far as I'm concerned." She ascended the short steps and walked back inside.

"Give yourself some credit, Chy," Seth said. "Her good deeds had to have come from somewhere."

Nicole turned to see her mother freeze in the doorway and give a meek smile, before departing.

"Your mother's a good woman," Seth said. "Never let her forget that."

"I won't," Nicole said. She leaned on him the way a little girl does to her father. "I promise."

CHAPTER 8

That evening, the group sat down for dinner in a dining room Nicole learned was called a horigotatsu, meaning the guests sat with their legs hanging over a recessed portion of the floor, at a table that reached their waists. It was an experience Nicole had seen others partake in New York, usually on the other side of restaurant glass, but one she had never experienced until now. Tonight's supper was ramen, served in a large bowl, mixed with pork belly, shiitake mushrooms, chopped seaweed, and hard-boiled eggs. Long, yellow noodles soaked up whatever flavors made up the delectable broth, and Nicole savored it all with fervor. She washed it down with a smooth and refreshing glass of Kirin and sat back with satisfaction.

"Daisuke," she said, "you've outdid yourself."

"Oh, don't thank me," Daisuke said. "Thank my cook, Omi. She's been serving food in this home since the 1860s."

Seth looked around with curiosity. "You have a chef living here? You could've fooled me."

"Ah," Daisuke said, pointing his chopsticks at him, "Omi is only with us in spirit. You see, she died some time ago, but she insists on making food for all who stay here."

Chyanne's glass froze mid sip. "She's a ghost?"

Daisuke nodded. "I've mentioned that I have psychic powers. That includes the ability to talk to spirits, and it turns out there's plenty of spirits in this house who are extremely hospitable." Daisuke smiled as he took a bite of his pork belly. "I knew them when they were alive, and I must have done something right because they wish to speak with me, even in death."

"Were they weredragons?" Seth asked.

Daisuke shook his head. "They were human parents of weredragon children, like Nicole's boyfriend's mother. They wanted to serve the sanctum however they could, in exchange for giving their children employment. And now, they tend to this home they've dwelled in for over a century."

Great, Nicole thought. *Just when I thought I'd get a good night's rest.*

"You oughtn't worry, though," Daisuke said, as though he read her mind. "They're friendly, and they leave the bedchambers when someone is sleeping in them. And before you ask, yes, they stay out of the bathrooms. But be careful what you say, because they have sensitive ears and they're eager to tell me everything."

Daisuke winked at Nicole and Chyanne, and Nicole felt her blood run cold. Their secret was out, and they were busted. If it wasn't giant, eight-headed dragons they had to worry about, it was ghosts who didn't know how to keep a secret. She felt like yelling at the walls, telling the nosy ghosts around her to mind their own business and stay dead.

"Well," Seth said, "I've seen and heard a lot of strange stuff in my life, but ghost maids are on a whole other level."

Daisuke responded in fashion, but Nicole heard none of it. Instead, her mind shifted to what she perceived to be a vibration along the soles of her feet, that gradually worked its way up the legs of the table and, eventually, the whole house. The trembling grew faster and more violent, shaking the foundation and causing the paper lights to flicker and sway. Objects fell off the shelves and their bowls and utensils were tossed around the table's surface like someone was kicking it from underneath.

"It's an earthquake," Daisuke said over the rumbling. "Just stay calm and it'll be over soon."

The night was shattered by a thunderous crack from outside. Nicole turned in the direction of the sliding door, only to see the peak of Mt. Sentsu split apart into a massive gorge that emitted a brilliant yellow light. Trees and rocks fell into the crack and were consumed by the light shining ever so brightly, filling the night sky with an amber haze. Nicole sprang to her feet and sprinted to the door as the light faded with the quake, and an eerie stillness descended upon the valley.

"Did you see that?" Nicole asked. Cautiously, she exited the house and glanced up at the mountain. Pieces of earth were still falling through the large crack, while wisps of what appeared to be smoke rose out of it like steam from a bath.

"I think it's time to investigate," Daisuke said. He stepped outside and transformed into his dragon form. Nicole was reminded of the serpentine dragons from ancient Asian art when she beheld his pale green scales and lanky, snake-like body. "Care to join me?"

"Now?" Chyanne asked. "Are you crazy?"

"Maybe I am," Daisuke said. "But maybe this is a sign, a sign that the Orochi is nigh."

Seth stepped forward and turned into his dragon form. "I say let's do it. Maybe it's already hatched and needs someone to imprint."

Nicole turned to Chyanne, who was still inside and looking apprehensive.

"Ah, screw it," Chyanne said, stepping out and changing into her dragon form. "At least I know if it kills us all I can say I told you so."

Nicole smiled, finally seeing her mother in her dragon form for the first time in so long. She gladly gave herself over to her dragon nature, and the quartet took off towards the mountain.

CHAPTER 9

It had been so long since Nicole had been in her dragon form with her mother. High above the Chugoku mountains, Nicole recalled happy memories of flying through the Northern Lights high above Nova Scotia. Chyanne looked a lot like Nicole, with her quartz scales and blue markings that created a pattern of stripes down her sides. The only thing missing were the scarlet scales under her wings, a feature Nicole inherited from her father. Instead, beneath Chyanne's wings a pattern of turquoise scales fanned out along their undersides, like the fins of a fish. Ahead of them, Daisuke coiled and dipped through the air, his whiskers flapping in the wind, his brilliant jade scales glimmering in the light from the moon. He was more stunning than any dragon Nicole had ever seen, and the fact that he was able to fly without wings was even more impressive. She wondered if all Asian weredragons were like him, and what other powers they may have that made westerners like her look basic.

"You've grown so much since the last time I saw you," Chyanne said, gliding next to her. Nicole glanced over and saw that she was actually larger than her mother in her dragon form. "I remember when you were a tiny dragonet, just barely able to flap your wings."

Nicole smiled. Most weredragons didn't turn until puberty, but Lucio's children turned around five or six. Nicole could not remember a time before she could turn, but she always remembered her mother being larger and superior to her. In her mind's eye, she still was.

"You're just as grand as I remember," Nicole said.

"Oh, stop," Chyanne replied. "The years of inhaling Hong Kong smog and smoking three packs a day have made me weak and feeble."

"Maybe this mountain air will do you good," Nicole said.

"Doubt it," Chyanne said. "Not until I quit cold turkey. You can blame your father for that. I never touched a pack of Lucky Strikes until I met him."

"By the way," Nicole said, "I found your old lighter. I didn't bring it because I wasn't sure how I could get it past the TSA, but it's still in my care."

Chyanne smiled meekly. "Thanks," she said. "Maybe you can give it to me if I ever travel to New York."

"I also found a picture of you," Nicole said, "inside a copy of *Oryx and Crake*."

"I love that book," Chyanne said. "Tried to get it signed by the author when you were three or so but missed it because you were sick."

"Oh," Nicole said, her voice dour. "Sorry."

"Comes with being a parent," Chyanne said. "You'll understand if you ever have children. By the way, what kind of picture was it?"

"You on your way to Hong Kong," Nicole said. "You were on the steps of a private plane."

"Ah, I know that picture," Chyanne said. "One of your father's associates snapped it. Don't know why . . . guess he thought I looked good. I thought at the time your father wanted to use it as a headshot for a mail-order bride service he ran on the side, but I never left Hong Kong so I guess I was never added."

Nicole was surprised at her mother's nonchalant response. It was as though the thought of being trafficked barely registered. Not even Nicole knew her father was involved with human trafficking, but to be honest, she ought not to be surprised.

"We're almost there," Daisuke called over his shoulder. They began their descent and landed at the edge of the crag. Nicole looked down into the dark abyss and kicked a loose boulder over the edge. She watched it be consumed by the darkness and listened for over a minute before it finally hit the rocky bottom. As she peered over the ledge, Chyanne reached out and held her back, as though she had forgotten that her daughter had wings.

"That's a long way down," Seth said. "Are you sure you want to go?"

"We should," Daisuke said. "But I haven't any idea how we'll be able to see. We may have to wait until daylight."

At that, Seth ignited a small flame from his nostrils, which he kept lit undisrupted.

Daisuke's eyes widened. "How on earth . . . ?"

"Spending years in the darkness forced me to adapt," Seth said. The flame continued even while he spoke.

"I can do that too," Nicole said. Her nostrils flared and she let out a small jet of flame, like the tip of a candle. "I can't do mine for as long, though."

"I can go ahead," Seth said, "to light the way. Nicole can take the rear."

"If you're up to it," Daisuke said. "Let's go slowly, though. We don't know what's down there."

"What's a few bats and spiders to us dragons?" Nicole asked.

"It's not typical cave critters I'm worried about," Daisuke said. "I'm more afraid of encountering a *yokai*."

"What the hell is that?" Seth asked.

"It means strange apparition," Daisuke said. "It's like a ghost or a demon, some good, some bad. I'm particularly worried about running into an *oni*, which are usually evil entities living in caves."

"I'm sure we'll be fine," Seth said. "I've seen tons of crazy stuff in my life, but never anything that was beyond my means of fighting back."

"*Kuso seiyō hito-me,*" Daisuke spat under his breath. "Okay, if you insist, please lead the way."

Seth took the plunge, falling through the crack in the ground and illuminating the sides of the deep cavern with his breath. Daisuke was close behind, followed by Nicole. But before Nicole could enter the cave, Chyanne put a hand on her shoulder.

"Nicole," she said, "if it's not too much, may I please hold onto your hand as we go? I know you're all grown up and all, but I just can't shake this feeling that we're about to walk into something horrible, and I want to make sure you're safe."

"Sure Mom," Nicole said, smiling. "Just don't tug too hard."

She offered her mom her left hand, and Chyanne took it as they leapt off the edge.

The temperature dropped as they plunged deeper into the earth. Nicole flapped her wings as wind whisked her face, causing her flame to burn sideways. She could see the edges of the cave, the layers of segmented rock, layers going back millions of years into the past. Nicole felt herself falling back in time, before dragons and humans came together and created the weredragons that roamed the earth today. The darkness was overwhelming, and soon, her light faded as the air grew moist and heavy. When they finally reached the ground, she could no longer keep her flame alive and was forced to exhale a cloud of smoke. Thankfully, Seth's flame continued to burn, and through its yellow light she could see the empty cavern around them. In front of him was a long passage, lined with stalactites and stalagmites, from which water dripped into small puddles within the grooves of the rock. But the thing everyone stared at, and the strangest sight so far, was a large archway built into the rock with Japanese letters carved into it:

強大なオロチを目覚めさせないでください。

"It says 'Do not awake the mighty Orochi'," Daisuke said. "We must be close to the egg if that's the case."

Nicole saw Seth narrow his eyes. "Have you ever catered to the thought that the Orochi doesn't want to be bothered? That maybe we should leave this thing alone."

"That's not what the legends say," Daisuke said. "They say the creature craves a guardian to call its parent." He turned to face Seth. "I say we provide that before your son does."

"If that's the alternative," Seth said, "I'd rather get a move on." He stared forward, and Daisuke followed. Nicole was about to do the same, when her mother grasped her shoulder.

"Remember," she whispered. "If we find the egg, we destroy it."

"Are you sure that's a good idea?" Nicole asked. "Think of the possibilities if we were able to control it."

"And think about what will happen if we can't," Chyanne said. "Streets of fire, seas of red, everyone we know and love dead or maimed."

Nicole started forward, with her mother close behind.

"I'm just saying," Chyanne said. "Legends have been known to lie. You know."

**

The trek down the cave was long and silent except for the constant dripping of water and the occasional bat. Occasionally, they would come across a post or a rock with kanji script written on it, but Daisuke would say they were nothing more than mile markers indicating how deep they were. Seth's flame continued burning and Nicole wondered how he hadn't passed out by now. Eventually, they reached a large cavern with a pool of clear water in the center, from which a small stream flowed towards the east through a smaller opening in the rocky wall.

"I wonder if this flows into the Hii River," Daisuke said, "a favorite haunt of the Orochi."

"At least we have an escape route if we get stuck," Seth said, "though that depends on how long you can hold your breath."

"I held my breath for an hour once," Nicole said. "Though, considering how far underground we are, it might be more than I can muster."

"Speak for yourself," Chyanne said. "Chain smokers aren't known for having the best lungs."

As they talked, Nicole saw Daisuke pick something up off the ground and hold it up to Seth's light. "Look," he said with a mixture of excitement and fear. They all crowded around Daisuke and peered down at the metal object in his hands. To Nicole, it looked like a small piece of pipe, barely larger than a thimble in Daisuke's talons.

"It's a bullet shell," Seth said. "Someone's been shooting in here."

Nicole stepped back and felt something rattle under her feet. She glanced down and noticed a twisted hunk of metal that was bent and contorted into a shape that was indescribable. But the barrel, trigger, and wooden stock betrayed any semblance of innocence, and revealed itself to be a rifle. She held it up to Seth's light.

"A Kalashnikov," Chyanne said, taking the rifle. "Probably an AKM or a close copy." She turned to Nicole. "Your father used to buy hundreds of these because they were cheap, and their ammunition was tough enough to pierce most dragon's scales."

"Those ain't no joke, either," Seth said. "I've been shot by them and they hurt like a mother."

"And someone obviously wasn't as phased," Chyanne said. "Maybe we ought to head back while we still have a chance.

As the others debated about what to do next, Nicole observed the surface of the water start to ripple with the sound of a far-off tremor. At first, she thought it might be another quake, but the more it rippled, the more it felt like the rhythmic footsteps of something very, very large. Soon, everyone fell silent as the footsteps made their way towards them in the cavern ahead.

"*Orochi no kakurega o midasu mono ga irudarou ka?*" said a deep, guttural voice that bounced off the walls and turned Nicole's blood to jelly.

"Who dares disturb the lair of the Orochi?" Daisuke repeated, his voice trembling.

There was movement in the light from Seth's flame, and from the shadows at the other end of the cavern, there emerged a monstrous creature. It was large, taller than any of them, with red skin, horns on its head, a wild black mane, and large, bulging eyes. It wore a leather loincloth around its waist, and a large club rested upon its shoulder.

"*Tawagoto*," Daisuke shrieked. "It's an oni."

"*Orokana doragon*," the oni said. "*Naze kita nodesu ka?*"

Daisuke stepped forward and cleared his throat. "*Anata ni gai wa nai to iu kotodesu. Watashitachiha kyūjō o sukutte kureru idaina Orochi o motomeru tan'naru tabibitodesu.*"

The oni laughed. "*Bakana yōji de kita nda ne. Ikite kono dōkutsu kara dete wa ikemasen.*"

"Anyone care to translate?" Seth whispered.

"I told him that we seek the wisdom of the Orochi," Daisuke said. "But he told us we're on a fool's errand and that we won't leave this cave alive."

The oni lowered his club and pointed it towards them. "*Kono shinseina basho ni seiyō hito o tsuretekuru nante, yokumo son'na kotoda! Hone kara niku o hagashite, hoka no yatsura to onajiyoni tabete yaru!*"

"What does that mean?" Nicole whimpered.

"It means he's going to eat us," Daisuke said. "In other words, we're *Fakku*."

The oni let out a howl and lunged towards them. Nicole bolted out of the way before its massive club could crush her. It came down just feet from her, shaking the whole cave under its might. She sprang to her feet and sent a jet of fire towards the oni, lighting its loincloth and scorching its belly. Seth and Daisuke did the same, bathing its back in flames. The oni turned and swung sideways, nearly striking the pair, and shattering a stalactite that dangled from above. Nicole was about to pounce, but her mother swooped in from above, dug her claws into its back, and sank her teeth into its neck. The oni screamed in pain and tried hitting Chyanne with its club, barely managing to graze her.

"*Bakana hakujin-domo yo!*" the oni screamed. "*Kono hiyō wa minasan ga haraimasu yo!*"

"*Kanojo wa hakujinde wa arimasen!*" Daisuke snapped. "*Anata wa mitame yori mo orokadesu!*" He lunged at the oni, his mouth aiming for its stomach, but the demon kicked him in midair, sending him flying into the side of the cavern with a crash. Seth leaped forward too, but the oni grabbed hold of Chyanne, pulled her off, and swung her towards him. Her body connected with his and Seth was thrown sideways, his body rolling across the floor of the cave.

The oni held Chyanne by the neck, his club at his side. Nicole saw her mother struggle, her claws digging into the meat of his massive forearm, but there was nothing she could do to free herself.

"*Mazu anata o tabemasu,*" the oni said, and opened its large, toothy maw.

"No!" Nicole screamed. She lunged towards the oni and sank her teeth into the back of its knee, deep into the hamstring. The oni cried and tried to kick Nicole off, dropping Chyanne in the process, who landed with a crash. The demon lost its footing, tripped and toppled forward, headfirst into the pool. Nicole let go when the water struck her, swallowing a mouthful of it in the process, and scrambled to swim her way back to the surface. But a sudden pain raced up her spine and she looked to see the oni grabbing her tail. Blood rose from multiple wounds across its body, and its face was contorted in a painful smile that almost resembled laughter. The oni sank further, and Nicole was pulled down along with it, the faint glimmer of Seth's light from above fading as the demon threatened to take her into a dark, watery tomb.

Nicole saw the oni's club following them and she reached for it, grabbing it by the handle. She pointed it downward and jabbed the oni in the face, striking its mouth and sending bits of teeth floating. She struck it again, hitting it on the nose, breaking it. She reared up again for a third time, and the oni held up its free hand to protect itself, but its fingers were broken beneath the heavy club, and its bulbous end struck it in the eye. The oni let go, its hands clutching its face, and sank to the bottom of the pool. Nicole emerged from the pool coughing and spitting up mouthfuls of water. Seth, Daisuke, and Chyanne were all gathered by the edge of the pool, each covered in cuts and bruises. As Nicole climbed out, her mother came to her side, patting her on her back and holding her close.

"Are you okay?" she asked.

Nicole coughed some more. "Yeah, I've always liked mineral water after a fight."

"Christ," Seth gasped. "You weren't kidding about the yokai."

"I told you," Daisuke said. "Those oni are no joke."

"They're not so bright either," Chyanne said. "Considering it called me a *Hakujin*."

"What does that mean?" Nicole asked.

"White person," Chyanne said. "He was only half right about you."

"It associates all westerners with *Hakujin*," Daisuke said. "That's why it was so aggressive, not just that we were intruding, but that westerners were here as well."

"Bit narrow-minded about it, eh?" Chyanne asked.

"Not all yokai are geniuses," Daisuke said. "Some are idiots, plain and simple, or *baka* as the Japanese call them."

"*Please don't bother the Orochi,*" said a voice that resembled a small boy.

"Who said that?" Nicole asked.

"Aw no," Seth groaned. "Not another one."

"*I mean you no harm,*" the voice said again. "*But please don't bother the Orochi.*"

Nicole noticed movement out of the corner of her eye and glanced into a dark corner at the back of the cavern, near the banks of the pool. A small dragon, no larger than a German Shepherd, stood close by, staring at them. It was green and serpentine, like Daisuke, but with wings, and a pair of wide, scarlet eyes. The dragon approached them and came into view, its little wings wobbling like the ears of a cat. Nicole approached the creature with caution; it looked innocent, almost cute, but looks could be deceiving.

"Who are you?" Nicole asked.

"My name is Ito," the creature said. "I was born when the eighth head of the original Orochi fell and was ordered by the warrior Susanoo to ward off all intruders. When Susanoo learned the Orochi had laid an egg, he told me it must never hatch, and that I must make sure no one finds it. I have lived here in this cave for over a thousand years, defending it with my army of yokai, to prevent a second Orochi from ever seeing the light of day."

Daisuke stepped forward. "But what of the legend? What of our quest to have the Orochi imprint on one of us?"

Ito turned to Daisuke. "It's just that, a legend, created by the original Orochi to trick mortals into bringing it back to life. The Orochi never dies, it only reincarnates inside an egg, waiting for someone to find it and free it from its shell. After which, it will continue to wreak havoc yet again." Ito turned to Nicole. "It wants you, Nicole Newheart, to free it, so you may be its bride."

Nicole blinked. This little creature that sounded like a first grader had just pulled the rug out from under her and left her questioning everything she knew.

"Why me?" Nicole asked. "Why would it want to marry me?"

Ito shook his head. "I know not. I only know its desire, not its motive."

"But what about Typhoon?" Seth asked. "He seeks the Orochi's egg too."

"He too has fallen for the Orochi's lies," Ito said. "He thinks because he created the original Orochi during his fight with Blizzard that he can control it. But the Orochi has a will beyond his imagination. The Orochi is playing him, and he will not find out until it is too late."

"So, we have to stop him from finding the egg," Chyanne says. "What if we destroy it before he gets there?"

Ito shook his head. "Impossible, not without the Kusanagi no Tsurugi, the sword taken from the corpse of the first Orochi.

Only with that sword can anyone think to defeat the Orochi, and trap its soul within its blade. Only this can prevent it from reincarnating again. But the Kusanagi has been locked away for thousands of years, and only the Imperial Family can access it. The last time it was removed from its hiding place was on the first day of May, 2019, during the coronation of Emperor Naruhito, at the beginning of the Reiwa Era."

"So, we have to prevent anyone from finding it?" Nicole said. "Seems like a tall order, especially since Typhoon seems so hellbent on claiming it as his own."

"Unfortunately," Ito said, "Typhoon's forces are dangerously close to finding the egg. Our only hope is to locate the Kusanagi sword and kill the Orochi before it kills all life in this world."

Suddenly, the pool erupted in a shower of blood and water. The oni emerged, angrier and more vicious than ever. It began screaming vulgarities in Japanese, the likes of which made Daisuke and Chyanne wince, and it glared at Nicole with eyes of pure hate. The oni stood on the banks, club in hand, and was about to strike . . .

But before it could do so, Ito began to sing a song so sweet, it stopped it in its tracks. The song, which was more like an operatic chant, was sung in a falsetto that reminded Nicole of the innocent voices of a youth choir. It seemed to have a supernatural effect on the oni, who was lulled into a hypnotic trance and stood there, its eyes wide and unblinking. Its arms sagging, it dropped its club with a thud, as Ito finished his song left Nicole hanging on his final verse.

"Wow," Nicole said. "How did you do that?"

"I command all yokai," Ito said. "It's one of my many powers."

Suddenly, a shot rang out through the cave, and the oni staggered backwards, a bloody wound bubbling from between its eyes. Two more shots followed, hitting the creature in the chest and stomach, and one more landed in the neck. The oni fell back into the water and vanished beneath the surface, as the shooter stepped forward into Nicole's field of view. It was Tauri, dressed exactly as he had been earlier that day, armed with a sniper rifle adorned with a wooden buttstock like the Kalashnikov from earlier. He slung the rifle over his shoulder, as a brigade of armed men approached him on his left and right.

"Beautiful song," Tauri said. "Where can I stream it?"

Ito stepped forward, his wings outstretched. "You have no business here, Tauri Allerton! Your mission is doomed to fail, and you and your men will face the consequences."

Tauri pointed an incriminating finger at the little dragon. "The only consequences are what'll happen if you talk to me like that again. Now put yourself to use and disable the rest of your minions so we can kill them with ease."

"No!" Nicole barked. She came to Ito's side, sheltering the little dragon with her wing. "You'll have to get through me first."

"And me," Seth said, joining her. "I helped bring you into this world, and goddammit I can take you out again."

"Fine," Tauri said, turning into his dragon form. He looked so much like Seth it was almost scary, with his tan scales, thick jaw, and clay markings. The only thing different were streaks of turquoise under his eyes and along the sides of his face. And he was considerably larger. "You want to play hardball, let's do it."

Before Nicole could respond, Tauri stepped forward and grabbed Ito by the neck and held him up high over everyone else. Nicole leap to try and save him, but Tauri turned and clobbered her with his tail, sending her flying into the wall. Chyanne, Seth, and Daisuke came to her side, as blood started to drip from her nose and trickle into her mouth.

Tauri turned to his men, while Ito struggled to free himself. "On my mark, shoot them."

The soldiers knelt and aimed their assault rifles. Nicole shut her eyes and readied herself for the wave of bullets about to strike her. It may take a while to kill a dragon with a gun, but she knew it was still possible, and extremely painful.

In the silence, Ito grunted. "Kappas of the Hii River. Heed my call. Save us!"

At that, the water behind them started to churn and wet footfalls echoed off the floor of the cavern. Nicole opened her eyes to see dozens of short, reptilian creatures that looked like a cross between a frog and a turtle. Their webbed hands were tipped with large claws, and their bodies were clad in thick, bony shells. They charged Tauri and his men. The soldiers opened fire, but the bullets were absorbed by their thick shells. More climbed upon Tauri and dug their claws into his scales, biting and scratching him, until the ground was wet with his blood. In trying to fend them off, he dropped Ito, who floated harmlessly to the ground.

"Quick," he said. "The river. We can follow it out of here while the Kappas hold them off."

Without hesitation, Ito dove into the stream and followed the current through the hole in the wall. Nicole took a deep breath and did the same, diving into the water and letting the current carry her through the cave. She felt the others behind her, and when she looked, she could see Seth, Daisuke, and her mother all close behind, holding onto each other so that they would not be separated. Nicole looked ahead and saw that Ito's scales were glowing a bright bioluminescent blue, his gleam casting a reflection on the smooth walls of the tunnel, which was swarming with more of those Kappas. Many of them were swimming back towards the cavern, their webbed hands pushing them up the current with ease to aid their comrades up top. Ahead, there was a bend in the tunnel, and Ito turned, gesturing for them to stop. They joined him and followed him up, where they emerged in a small air pocket above the curve.

"We don't have long to go," Ito said. "The current will take us out of here in less than an hour. The important thing is to not lose sight of me, and don't let yourself run into the wall, lest it slows you down."

"What about the Kappas?" Daisuke asked. "Should we be worried about them?"

"As long as they see you are no threat to me, they won't attack you," Ito said. "They're powerful swimmers, and they'll move out of your way with ease. Besides, the closer we get to the mouth of the Hii, the less numerous they'll become." He gave everyone one last look. "Is everyone ready?"

"Not quite," Chyanne said. "I can't hold my breath for long."

"Then you ride the current with me," Ito said. "I know this place better than anyone else, and I can get you out of here faster. But the rest of you can't stay behind too long. This is the only air pocket on the way, and if you slip up, you're done for."

Nicole nodded and took a few deep breaths. She tried not to think about the ordeal she was about to endure but instead focused on the freedom that would greet her on the other side. "Okay," she said. "I'm ready."

When everyone else had prepared, they all dove back down into the water, and rode the current forward. Nicole used her hands and feet to propel herself, keeping her eyes locked on Ito and her mother, not wanting to lose sight of them for a second. She passed numerous Kappa, more than she could count. The strange creatures stared at her through unblinking, reptilian eyes. She noticed that all of them had hair on their heads, except for a spot on the dome of their skulls that looked sunken in, like the inside of a bowl. She made a mental note to inquire about it later and pushed forward, looking back on occasion to make sure Seth and Daisuke were still behind her. Sure enough, they were, and Daisuke resembling an eel even more while swimming through the water.

Nicole looked ahead, and her heart sank. Her mother, who had until now swum with Ito, was now clutching his tail, relying on him to guide her forward. Furthermore, Nicole could tell she was in some kind of distress. She paddled lethargically and struggled to avoid hitting the walls of the tunnel. Nicole paddled faster, and noticed her mother's chest was puffed out; she was struggling to hold her breath. Nicole fought the urge to panic and grabbed her mother's talon, gripping it like she had when the two descended the cave earlier. Chyanne looked at Nicole, her eyes dazed, her face pale. It was obvious to Nicole her mother was a few seconds away from drowning.

Nicole gripped her mother's face, pressed her lips against hers, and exhaled into her mouth. Even in her dragon form, Chyanne's breath tasted like nicotine. Nicole exhaled like someone performing CPR, then let go, and put her talons on Chyanne's mouth to keep any of the air from leaving. Chyanne looked dazed, but alive, and nodded at Nicole with a sign of thanks and approval. Nicole continued holding onto her mother until finally, the moonlight cut through the water ahead, and they surfaced into the crisp air of a late Summer's night.

CHAPTER 10

Nicole pulled herself out of the water and collapsed. She never felt more relieved to be on dry land, and didn't care if she never swam again. She heard the others leave the water, and her mother gulping mouthfuls of air like it was water and she had been in the desert for days. Nicole looked up and craned her head towards her mother, who was clutching her chest while Ito stood next to her, his little talon on her back.

"Are you okay, Mom?"

"Yeah," Chyanne exhaled. "I'm just . . . going . . . to throw out all my Lucky Strikes . . . and tomorrow morning, I'm walking to the nearest store and buying a pack of nicotine gum."

"You're a smoker?" Ito asked.

"Two packs a day, for twenty years," Chyanne said. She flopped onto her stomach and buried her face in her hands, prompting Nicole to sprint to her side. "I felt myself dying in there, baby. I saw bits and pieces of my life, and I thought I was going to die. I saw . . . I saw your birth."

Chyanne sobbed and Nicole rubbed the area between her shoulder blades. "It's okay," she said. "We made it."

"No," Chyanne said, looking up. "My job as a mother is to protect you, and I couldn't even do that because of my own vices. I'm quitting tonight. To hell with the tobacco and the booze. It's over. I'll never touch a cigarette or a bottle again."

"I'll help you, Mom," Nicole said. "If you let me."

"I will, baby," Chyanne said. "I will."

"Nicole," Ito said, "you're bleeding."

Nicole felt the spot on her face where Tauri had struck her and ran her talons along a deep gash that was moist with blood.

"It's no biggie," Nicole said. "Just a cut."

"No, let me help," Ito said. He stepped forward, and Nicole noticed his eyes were moist with tears.

"It's not worth crying over," Nicole said. "Seriously, I've had worse."

But Ito ignored her. With the talon on his index finger, he gathered a single tear, then reached up and dabbed it upon Nicole's cheek. She felt a strange tingling sensation, followed by a warmth, and when Ito removed his finger, the wound was gone. Nicole felt around for it, but other than the dried specks of blood that were left behind, there was no sign. Not even a scar. Ito smiled, his little wings flapping with jubilation.

"Some things are worth crying over," he said with a wink.

"Wish you were with us in New York," Seth said. "Had a lot of injuries after the dust settled."

"I wish I had," Ito said. "But I cannot leave this place for long. So long as the egg exists, I must protect it. And now, I must tell as many as possible about the danger it poses, before Typhoon and Echo find it."

Daisuke hung his head and sighed. "This was all for nothing," he said. "I dragged you all here and put everyone in so much danger, all because of a lie."

"Don't be hard on yourself," Ito said. "Many have fallen for the Orochi's lies over the years. At least you learned the truth before it was too late."

Daisuke looked up. "I must tell the others in the sanctum, warn them that we need to change our views and our objectives."

"I'll help you," Ito said. "If they won't believe you, they'll believe me, even if I have to summon an army of Kappas to bite them in the *Ketsu no ana*."

Daisuke smiled. "I do appreciate your assistance, though I don't think it'll be that drastic."

Nicole stepped forward to the edge of the river. "Someone should scout the area, find out where Echo's camp is located and the size of their operation." She glanced back at the group. "I'll do it."

"And I'll come with you," Chyanne said. "You need backup, a helping hand. I know I might not be in the best of health, but I won't slow you down."

Nicole nodded. She knew better than to argue with her mother after all they had been through as of late.

"Do you ladies need help?" Seth asked.

"I don't think so," Nicole said. "I think we can handle ourselves. You go along with Daisuke and Ito, protect them and back them up."

"I appreciate this," Daisuke said. "But please, don't put yourselves in danger for my sake."

"We won't," Nicole said, extending her wings. She turned to her mother. "Ready Mama?"

Chyanne smiled and extended her wings too. "Since the day you were born."

They flapped their wings and ascended into the air.

"Good luck!" Ito said. "Give the yokai my regards. I'll make sure they don't attack you."

* * *

The night air lapped against Nicole's scales as she flew, scanning the forests and mountains for any sign of life. But it was as dark below as it was above, and the more they flew, the more Nicole began to doubt they would find anything. She could sense her mother felt the same way, judging by her antsy motion with which her wings flapped. Nicole strained her eyes, forcing them to cut through the dark in a desperate bid to see anything, be it the headlights from a car or a flashlight, but to no avail.

"They gotta be here somewhere," Nicole said.

"Unless they all went underground," Chyanne said. "Or

they're using camouflage to hide from above. Makes sense, especially for a mercenary group with questionable legal status."

Nicole frowned. "Maybe we should wait till morning," she said.

"Nah, this is probably our best bet," Chyanne said. "It'll be harder for them to see us from above, making us less of an open target. Unless, of course, they have thermal scopes, then we're screwed six ways till Saturday."

Nicole tensed; she hadn't thought of thermal scopes. Did Tauri have one on his sniper rifle? Could he shoot her out of the sky? Instinctively, she flew higher, and in zigzags in case anyone was tracking them.

"Scary shit we're up against," Chyanne said. "Mercenaries, yokai, evil world-destroying dragons. If I knew we'd get involved in any of this, I'd have taken a wad of cash out of my neighbor's mattress and booked a flight to New York."

Nicole laughed. "Fate would've grounded you somehow," she said. "Something tells me that whatever led us here did so for a reason."

"Let's just hope that reason is a good one," Chyanne said. "And not another of the Orochi's tricks."

"So, what's your thought on the egg now?" Nicole said. "You still want to destroy it?"

"I say we leave it alone," Chyanne said. "Seal off the cave and tell everyone with a conscience to piss off. But that's probably too much to ask."

"Why do you say that?" Nicole asked.

"Because people are stupid. Weredragons are stupid. The whole of the human race is populated by ignorant boneheads who'd gleefully sell their children's future for a few dollars more. The sea levels rise higher, the poor become poorer, democratic institutions come apart at the seems, and the bastards who can actually make a difference choose not to because suffering is profitable. The world as we know it is already teetering on a cliff, and the ones in charge think the best course of action is to kick the can over the edge and watch the streets burn."

Nicole opened her mouth to speak but couldn't find a way to refute her mother's words. Her mother had experienced so much pain in her long life, more than even Nicole could imagine. Nicole realized if she had been in the same situation, she would probably find herself agreeing.

The silence of the night was shattered by an ear-splitting crack, startling Nicole. Her eyes darted from side to side, looking for the source of the shot, fearing the worst. She noticed the glimmer of headlights down below, and she tensed up.

"We're under attack!" Nicole screamed. "We're–"

"Baby, relax," Chyanne said. "It's just the sound of an exhaust backfiring." Her mother reached out to keep her in place, and pointed down to the pair of taillights wobbling along a dirt path at the base of the mountain. The vehicle's exhaust backfired again, and Nicole eased.

"Let's check it out," Nicole said. "Maybe they're with Echo."

"Sure, but let's keep our distance," Chyanne said.

They dove a few meters behind the vehicle and clung to a large tree overlooking the dirt path. In the dim light, Nicole could make out the profile of an old sport utility vehicle, with a large cargo area adorned with dark, rounded windows.

"Looks like a 40 series Toyota Land Cruiser," Chyanne said. "Another favorite of your father due to its reliability. It's a troop carrier, or 'troopy' as it's also called, and," Chyanne sniffed the air, "it's a diesel."

"Seems suspicious," Nicole said. "Why would anyone be driving this late at night, and in a troop carrier no less."

"The troopy was sold to the general public," Chyanne said. "It's not as special as it sounds, and it could be a police officer or park ranger doing his rounds."

"I still think it's worth following," Nicole said. "Just for giggles. It could be nothing, but we can't be too careful."

Nicole and Chyanne landed and crawled along the forest floor, following the Land Cruiser closely. It wasn't hard to do; the vehicle lumbered along the uneven trail at a snail's pace, its taillights bobbing over obstacles. Eventually, the truck followed the road down an embankment that led to a small meadow. There at the bottom, hidden by the canopy of trees, was a camp. Large tents had been set up, their tops covered in camouflage awnings. A diesel generator hummed from somewhere, powering electric lights that cast a dim glow. Several large gas canisters were stacked upon a pallet, covered with netting as well. The Land Cruiser was greeted by armed guards, carrying assault rifles tipped with bayonets that glimmered in the artificial light. It pulled to a stop and the rear doors opened. Several heavily armed soldiers stepped out.

Nicole and Chyanne waited and watched from behind an outcropping of rocks.

"Do you see Tauri anywhere?" Chyanne asked.

Nicole strained her eyes. "No," she said. "None of them look familiar. Maybe if I can get closer . . ."

Cautiously, she stepped over the boulder and crept towards the camp. She was almost able to make out what the soldiers were saying, when she heard a click under her front right foot. Nicole froze.

"Mom," Nicole said. "Can you come here please?"

"Baby, what is it?" Chyanne asked.

"I think I stepped on something . . . serious," she said.

Chyanne dashed over to her side, lit a nearby branch with her flames, looked down, and gasped.

"What is it?"

"Honey," Chyanne said. "Try not to panic, but you've stepped on a landmine."

"Oh god," Nicole said beginning to hyperventilate "Mom, what's going to happen? It can't hurt me that much, can it?"

"I don't know," Chyanne said. "It looks like a tank mine. They probably put it here to deter vehicles, possibly other dragons."

Nicole became faint. Her heart raced and her legs, tail, and wings felt numb. She could almost feel the burn of the blast, the maiming she would receive.

"Mom, I can't die like this," she said, her tears stinging her eyes. "There's got to be a way. There's—"

"Hang on," Chyanne said. She stamped out her torch and stepped back. "Stand still. Do you hear me?"

Nicole nodded and shut her eyes. She waited, but nothing happened. For a brief, terrible moment, she thought her mother had abandoned her to save her own scales. But before she could burst into tears and plead with the dragon mother to spare her, she heard her mom's wing beat, and she was shoved to the left. There was a blast. Nicole felt fire lick her scales and bits of shrapnel whiz past her. She landed hard on the ground, and her mother landed on top of her. Nicole waited, her ears ringing, the feeling coming back into her limbs. She opened her eyes, and realized her mother had her in a bear hug. She could smell blood, but she didn't know where she was injured.

It was then she realized the blood was not coming from her.

"Mom?" she asked.

No answer. Chyanne made a face that looked like a painful grimace, before she slumped over, her body motionless.

CHAPTER 11

A barrage of shots rang out across the forest. Bullets whizzed and zoomed over Nicole's head, shearing the bark off the surrounding trees and showering her with splinters. Nicole heaved her mother off her and pulled her behind a nearby rock. A groan from Chyanne indicated that she was still alive, but seriously hurt.

"Okay, Mom," Nicole said. "Thanks for saving me. Now, I'm going to return the favor, but I'm going to need you to help me out a bit."

"Ehh," Chyanne said.

She took her mother by the arm and slung her over her shoulder, pulling her up on her back feet and carrying her in the direction from whence they came. As they did, three large utility task vehicles roared over the hill, tearing up the terrain as they went. Ridden by armed men, the vehicles resembled ATVs, but larger. The UTVs encircled Nicole and Chyanne, and the soldiers shot at them.

"Ouch!" Nicole screamed as the bullets struck her scales, stinging her like hornets. She laid her mother down. "Keep your head down, Mom."

"Emm, hmmm," Chyanne replied.

Nicole heard the sound of a large weapon being cocked as she turned to face their attackers. Atop one of the UTVs was a mounted machine gun, its bullets dangling from a belt, and a soldier aiming it at her. The driver accelerated as the gunner pulled the trigger, letting loose a wave of bullets that tore the foliage and cut the air inches from Nicole's face. Before it could get close enough, Nicole dove out of its way and swung her tail, striking the vehicle in the roll cage. The gunner went flying backwards, while the driver hit the gas and slammed into a tree.

"One down," Nicole said. She had hardly spoken before searing, burning pain raced up her spine. At first she thought they were being attacked by a dragon, but when turned she saw another UTV fitted with a mounted flamethrower. Nicole ducked as another jet of fire lit up the night and lunged. Before the soldier even had time to readjust, Nicole was on top of him, crushing the driver beneath her. She grabbed him in her mouth and shook, breaking every bone in his body, and tossed him aside, wrapping his body around a tree trunk.

A third engine revved, and Nicole turned to face it. The driver was circling Nicole, keeping his distance and accelerating so that she couldn't breathe fire on him. Nicole growled; she hated tricks like this, and the frustration bubbled up in her throat. She summoned some fire from her breath, aimed at a spot of ground in front of the off-roader, and sent a fireball its way. The vehicle was engulfed in flames, igniting the gas tank and causing the grenades on the driver's vest to detonate. A screaming, popping fireball, he veered into the forest to explode and smolder.

"Oh no you don't," Chyanne said. Nicole turned to see her mother grab a soldier between her talons and twist him in two, shattering his spine and immobilizing him. He dropped the grenade launcher he was holding and collapsed into a heap at her feet.

Nicole approached her mother. "How are you feeling?"

Chyanne cracked her neck and shook the dirt and debris off of her. "I've been better," she said. "There's a ringing in my ear and a pain in my neck, but it's nothing too serious."

"You sure about that?" Nicole asked. "You're walking kind of funny."

Chyanne tried to approach Nicole but staggered. Nicole dashed forward to catch her. "Maybe it's worse than you thought," she said. "Can you fly at all?"

Chyanne extended her wings and immediately cried out in pain.

"Holy shit," she said. "That hurts like a mother."

Out in the distance, the sound of engines roared.

"Come on," Nicole said. "We need to get you back to Ito. Climb on my back, and we'll fly to town."

"Are you sure?" Chyanne asked. "*Can* you carry me?"

"Sure," Nicole said. She lowered herself and allowed Chyanne to climb onto her shoulders. Chyanne wrapped her arms around her daughter's neck and planted her heels against the inside of her thigh like a jockey. Nicole extended her wings, flapped and, with much effort, ascended into the sky.

Up above, the night remained unchanged. The stars still twinkled their vibrant luminescence in the dark, mystical sky. Their pursuers' sounds faded as they reached higher, but the more Nicole flew, the more she felt the pain from the many bullet wounds that were lodged under her scales like splinters. She felt blood trickle down her arms and legs, and she grew weaker with each wingbeat.

Eventually, Nicole had to land. She touched down upon a clearing, its lush grass glowing in the moonlight. She knelt to let her mother off and exhaled as the hours caught up to her all at once.

"Are *you* okay?" Chyanne asked.

"No," Nicole said. "I'm sorry, Mom. We're going to have to go by foot."

Chyanne put a talon on her shoulder. "Let's sleep here tonight. We'll continue in the morning. Perhaps by then, someone will send a search party out for us."

Nicole collapsed and laid her head upon the grass. She did not want to admit how good the thought of sleeping felt to her. Part of her felt ashamed that she couldn't carry her mother further. But then again, everyone has their limits.

Chyanne knelt next to Nicole and spread her wing over her, covering her like a blanket. "You did well today, child of mine. I'm proud of you."

"Thanks," Nicole said. Her eyes grew heavy as she sank into the grass, letting the sounds of the night carry her off and make her pain melt away. She fell into a dreamless sleep, and did not wake for as long as the stars twinkled above her.

CHAPTER 12

ome to me.

The voice was a whisper, barely audible over the ambient noise of a forest at dawn. Nicole opened her eyes, but they were alone. She and her mother hardly moved since the night before, and Chyanne's wing was still draped over her. It was a damp, overcast day, Nicole could see, and even now she could smell the faint scent of rain in the air. Nicole laid there for a moment, listening to her mother's breathing, recalling a time when she was a young girl, and her mother would nudge her awake on a Saturday morning. The memory, and the feeling, gave Nicole a sense of safety that she hadn't felt in over a decade. She closed her eyes to doze off again, and she probably would have been successful, had it not been for her bladder urging her to attend to nature's call. Begrudgingly, Nicole left the security of her mother's wings and ventured into the forest to relieve herself.

As she walked, she couldn't help but feel she was being watched. The forest was dense, full of vines and bushes, and in the distance the trees melted into a blur of greenery that seemed to her an unscalable wall. Anything could be out here, watching her at her most vulnerable. Quickly, Nicole wandered over to a nearby embankment, did what she had to do, and scampered back up the hill.

And that's when she saw it, a red blinking light, between

the roots of a tall, thin sycamore. It didn't dawn on Nicole what it might be, but when she took a closer look, she noticed the smooth, glass disc, surrounded by thick, green plastic, and realized it was a camera. Nicole narrowed her eyes; was this a trap set by Echo, or some hunter's contraption? Either way, it seemed to be recording her, and at a time like this, smiling for the camera was out of the question. Nicole looked side to side, making sure no one else was watching, then, she coiled her index finger against the side of her thumb, and gave the camera a swift flick. The whole thing shattered at once, falling to the ground in bits and pieces. Nicole stepped on the part she thought contained the SD card, making sure the mud was caked into the various crevices.

As she turned, a gentle buzz cut through the ambiance of the forest. She turned her head to face it but saw nothing except the treetops over her. It sounded like a power saw as it drew closer, and Nicole stiffened. Then, out of the corner of her eye, there was movement. Nicole turned to see a quad-copter drone hovering a few feet off the ground, a camera pointed at her. Like the trap cam, it too was clad in camo paint, but there seemed to be more intent behind this drone, as it buzzed and whizzed around Nicole, its aperture widening and narrowing as it focused in on her. She waited for the drone to come to a halt, then she sent a jet of fire out of her mouth and engulfed it in flames. It fell to the ground where it smoldered and melted, sparks shooting from its sides as it sputtered its last bits of life.

From out in the distance, Nicole heard the roar of engines and the grinding of dirt under wheels. She saw birds evacuate the trees in waves and deer awaken from their rest to leap away. She felt the ground shake as a throbbing wave of mechanical fury came up to meet her. She leapt and flew through the trees, praying her mother was awake and able to fly. When she reached Chyanne, she was awake, alert, and when she saw Nicole overhead, relieved.

"There you are," she said. "What the hell is going on?"

"I don't know," Nicole said, "but we've gotta get out of here.

Can you fly?"

"Kinda," Chyanne said, extending her wings with a wince. "I don't know if I can go very fast, though."

Nicole looked over her shoulder. "I'll try to lure them away from here, while you make your way back to town."

"What are you talking about?" Chyanne said. "You don't even know what's causing that noise."

"Yeah, but I can haul ass a whole lot faster than you," Nicole said. "Besides, they probably want me more than you anyway."

"Exactly," Chyanne said. She grabbed Nicole by the shoulders. "God only knows what Echo has in store. Nicole, don't do this. Get out of here and don't worry about me."

Nicole brushed her mother's talons off of her. "I'm not going to leave you to die, not after all this time. Now go and alert the others, while I hold them off for as long as I can."

She leapt and flew towards the rumbling, all while her mother protested and pleaded. Nicole knew her mother thought it wrong to let her daughter throw herself into harm's way for her sake, but leaving her mother to be captured or killed was out of the question. No matter how little Chyanne valued herself, Nicole would never abandon her to their enemies.

The fumes of burning gasoline filled Nicole's nose and she grappled a nearby tree, clinging to its trunk. She locked her eyes onto a rounded hill, beyond which the thundering roar grew louder and closer. Then, they all came at once. Cutting through the foliage and tearing the forest floor was the nose of a Suzuki Jimny, then another, and another. Two dozen or so black, boxy SUVs cleared the hurtle with ease and floored it towards Nicole's vantage point. Each one was topped with a machine gun, commanded by a gunner that sat behind a rotating turret. Each one was fitted with heavy off-road modifications, like thick bumpers and meaty tires that looked like they could drive over Daisuke's Kei car with ease. They were joined by a single Toyota Hilux pickup, also black, and topped with a harpoon gun. The harpoon itself was steel tipped, with razor-sharp edges and nasty hooks at the bottoms, meant to dig into flesh and never let go.

Nicole froze. Her expectations for Echo Group were high, but nothing like this.

The sound of gunfire jolted Nicole back to reality. She let go of the tree and darted to the right, just as a hail of bullets struck the part of the trunk where she had clung and sheared the branches clean off. Nicole flew for her life, and emerged over a grassy meadow where she could finally stretch her wings and fly at top speed.

She turned behind her to see the Jimnys sail over the top of the hill and land hard onto the lush grassland. Their spiked treads of their tires ripped up huge chunks of earth with impunity. Their engines whined like the squealing of an angry cat, and their guns rattled like a blown speaker. Nicole beat her wings faster as she summoned some fire from her chest. She let loose a fireball which struck the ground at the foot of the caravan, singeing a few and scattering the rest. But they quickly reformed and charged forward. Nicole knew if she paused long enough to deliver a well-aimed jet of fire, they would poke her wings full of holes and tear her scales to ribbons. She thought of her stepsister, Delany, and how her wings erupted into bloody pockmarks as a National Guard chopper shot her out of the sky.

Nicole turned forward and almost collided with an osprey tiltrotor that was flying low over the field. She swooped, her tail brushing the underside. She felt the chopper bank and follow her, its two large propellers clipping the air with a rhythmic hum. She couldn't tell much about the helicopter, only that it was big, green, and had large guns on its wings and underside that could ground her forever.

Nicole's heart raced, her chest rose and fell, her wings flapped until they ached. She wanted to get as far away from this place as possible, escape these madmen and their gear. She felt weak, small even. In the eyes of these men, she was but a lizard who posed no more of a threat to them than the average vermin.

Suddenly, there was a sharp jolt of pain from her lower extremities. Nicole screamed and felt something tug at her. She looked down and noticed a harpoon sticking out of her hip, its barb embedded deep in her scales. The harpoon connected to a wire, which led to the Hilux down below. Nicole turned to face her attacker, grasping the spot where it punctured her, and tried to pull away. But the driver threw the vehicle in reverse and stepped on the gas, pulling the wire taut and jerking Nicole down. Nicole grasped the wire, struggling against the might of the truck as all four wheels kicked up mounds of mud and the winch on the harpoon began to retract. Nicole felt the harpoon pull at her scales as her wings flapped helplessly. To her right, the osprey hovered, observing the scene like a spectator, while the trucks below gathered beneath her like vultures. Their guns fired, and try as she might, some of the bullets found their target. Nicole couldn't tell how many times she was hit, just that she was bleeding profusely and the grass below her was moist with blood.

Something, or someone, had to give, and Nicole was sure as hell not going to let it be her.

Nicole grasped the tip of the barb, dug her talons into the wound, and pulled. She bit her lip to keep from screaming as the pain tore through her like lightning bolts. She unhooked loops of flesh from around the barb with one hand and pulled with the other, causing a stream of blood to cascade down her leg. She looked away from the wound and took deep breaths, which she hoped would keep her from going into shock, but it didn't work; a sudden sleepy feeling came over her. She gave the harpoon one final pull, and the barb dislodged.

Willing herself to focus, Nicole glared at the driver of the Hilux with venom in her eyes. The gunner loosened the slack in the wire, but Nicole wasn't having any of it. She grasped the wire, wound it around her hands, and pulled. The truck lifted off the ground and swung like a yoyo at the end of the string. She turned towards the osprey, which was starting to back away, and arched the wire upward, aiming the Hilux at its underside. The Hilux collided with the osprey, detonating into a ball of flames. The blades detached from the top, spinning aimlessly into the air, as the fiery wreck dropped to earth and exploded on impact.

The trucks on the ground scattered away from the inferno, as Nicole sent a jet of flames into their midst. She lit them, burned them, watched their metal husks smolder and their drivers try to escape, only to be consumed by fire. Nicole breathed every ounce of fire she had onto the trucks, until every last one was engulfed, and the valley was turned to a pile of flaming rubble and black smoke.

Nicole smothered the fire in her throat and glided to the ground. She landed at the edge of the inferno and watched as flames coiled around shattered windshields and gaping engine bays. She looked down at her feet and saw the barb, coated in her blood and bits of flesh. She reached down and felt the wound, felt the blood still spewing from the fleshy hole in her scales, and grew faint. She felt her legs grow weak and she stumbled. As she did, she saw the door of a Jimny lying just feet from her, its metal coating warped and blackened by flames. She reached out, grabbed it with the tip of her talons, rolled onto her back, and pressed it against her wound.

"Goddammit!" Nicole cried. The pain, mixed with the smell of her burning scales, nearly made her pass out. But the more she pressed, the more the pain subsided, until the wound hardened and bled no longer. Nicole removed the door and again felt the wound, now a crusty scab on the side of her body.

Nicole pulled herself up and crawled away. She made it almost to the side of a gravel path, a dozen or so meters away from the valley, before collapsing with exhaustion. She knew she had lost too much blood to continue forward. She fought against her impulses, struggling to stay awake, but the urge to rest and let her body heal was overwhelming. She let out a long sigh and rolled onto her back, as gray clouds rolled in, and the first drops of rain pelted her face. High above her, she saw the outline of dragon's wings descending towards her. As the dragon came closer, she hoped that it was Seth, or Daisuke, or even her mother. But as her eyes grew heavy, she noticed features on him that she did not recognize, until it dawned on her.

Tauri landed next to Nicole and lifted her into his arms. He looked into her eyes with concern and appeared to examine her for any signs of life.

"Damn it," he said. "I told them not to be too rough with her."

"She'll live," said a deep, husky voice Nicole had never heard before. "I've seen worse, experienced worse. Give her a few hours and a healing incantation and she'll be back to normal."

"Are you sure?" Tauri said. "If she's not able to break the egg–"

"Then we'll make her," the voice said. The outline of a head appeared on her right, a dark, scaly one with a pair of bright, red eyes.

"Typhoon," Nicole exhaled.

"See?" Typhoon said. "She's not dying, just in shock. She needs to rest it off, then we can introduce her to the wonderful world of surrogate motherhood."

"Wha..."

"That's right, little one," Typhoon said. "We need you for a very important job. Now rest, because you've got a long journey ahead."

Typhoon's eyes continued to burn inside of Nicole's eyelids long after she passed out. They haunted her dreams and filled her sleep with an all-consuming sense of dread.

And the voice called out to her again. *Come to me. Be with me. Free me.*

CHAPTER 13

Nicole awoke with a start. She could not move: her arms and legs were hogtied with chains, a muzzle was placed on her mouth, and a metal clamp pressed against her neck. It was dark, aside from the amber glow of lightbulbs dangling from wires from a rocky ceiling. She assumed she was inside a cave, given the damp rocky walls and the thick, musty air that coated her lungs like soup. There were voices in the shadows, speaking in Russian or a similar dialect that Nicole didn't understand. She noticed movement from her side and craned her head to get a glimpse. There, emerging from the shadows, was a dragon with green scales, and a potbellied man in military fatigues. As they drew closer, Nicole could make out a 'Z' stitched into the front of the man's outfit, which bulged over the edge of his cargo pants as he waddled.

"Ah, you're awake," the dragon said, in a thick Russian accent. "How are you feeling? Head hurt at all?"

"She can't talk if she has that thing on her face," the man replied.

"I know that, Tokarev," the dragon spat. "I have eyes, you know."

"Just checking, Nikolai," Tokarev said. "You've spent a long time in cave. Not good for your eyes."

Nikolai reached forward to grasp Nicole's muzzle, while Tokarev took out a large remote from his breast pocket.

"Don't do anything stupid, Pocahontas," Tokarev said. "Around your neck is a shock collar. One push of my button, and fifty-thousand volts of electricity will fry you from the inside out. Understand?"

Nicole nodded as Nikolai removed her muzzle.

"Where am I?" she asked.

"About three miles on the side of the mountain," Nikolai said. "Just down the passage is the entrance to the main cavern, and beyond that, is the egg of the Orochi."

"It sits behind a pair of thick, stone doors," Tokarev said. "I say we should blow it to hell and back, but bossman says that we have to wait for you."

"Why me?" Nicole said.

"Well," Nicolai said, "other than the fact that blasting it with dynamite will cause the cave to collapse, if the Orochi has chosen you to be its *mat'*, only you can open the door."

"But it's all a lie," Nicole said. "The Orochi wants someone to break it out of its egg, so it can be freed and conquer the world. You're all walking into a trap."

Tokarev shrugged. "Hey, we just do what we're told and get paid. If an eight-headed dragon wants to burn the whole world to a crisp, let him, just as long as my check clears."

"Money will be useless if the Orochi is freed," Nicole said.

Tokarev yawned and took out a flask. "Money will always talk if there's bullshit to walk." He took a swig, chugging his brew in thick, greedy gulps.

"Jesus, Milkava," Nikolai said, "it's only ten in the morning."

Tokarev lowered his flask and scowled at his partner. "What did I tell you about calling me by that name? I'm Tokarev, like my pistol." He took out an onyx handgun with a long, smooth slide, and waved it around with reckless abandon. "My grandfather shoved this down the throat of a Nazi in Stalingrad during the war."

"Bah," Nikolai said. "Your grandfather spent the war in a brothel, only to come out to steal vodka from the Red Army."

"*Ekh, idi k chertu ty, kazak!*" Tokarev snapped. "*YA*

zanimalsya seksom s tvoyey mater'yu i zabral yeye trusiki domoy v kachestve suvenira."

Nikolai's nostrils flared. *"A ya trakhnul tvoyu sestru i otpravil yeye domoy k mamochke, pokrytoy moim semenem."*

Nicole rolled her eyes; she was getting real sick of not being able to understand anybody. She watched the two men bicker, as Tokarev flashed his precious gun and spewed insults that, Nicole assumed, were laced with vile puns. Part of her hoped the gun would go off, and the bullet would ricochet off the cavern ceiling and strike the greedy hunk of flesh square in the jowls. Or at least that Nikolai would tire of his partner's insults and end him. Given neither of these were likely to happen, all Nicole could do was sit, wait, and ruminate on her situation. Her bindings were strong, stronger than the ones used to hold her to the floor of her father's cargo plane months before. She could not burn through them, and they were far too thick for her to break. On top of that, the collar cut off the fire in her neck, preventing her from frying her captors. She was stuck, watching two morons argue about god knows what, as the injuries she'd acquired over the last few days suddenly decided to let themselves be known and make her even more uncomfortable.

"Will you two shut up already!" Nicole snapped. "What are you waiting for anyway?"

"We're waiting for the bossman to come and give us our orders," Nikolai said. "He told us to sit and watch you and make sure you don't do anything stupid."

"Like I can do anything now," Nicole said. "If you haven't noticed by now, you have me tied like a damn pig roast. I can't even scratch my own ass!"

"Sorry, Pocahontas," Tokarev said. "Tauri and Typhoon gave us our orders, and we've both got debts to pay."

"And stop calling me Pocahontas," Nicole snapped. "She wasn't even part of the same tribe I'm descended from. Don't you know I'm from Canada and she was born in Virginia? Or does Echo Group not care if its members have literal shit for brains?"

"Why you . . ." Tokarev said. But before he could say or do

anything in retaliation, a white light appeared at the end of the cavern. Nicole looked up to see a silver SUV approach them, its thick wheels maneuvering over the uneven ground with ease. Nicole realized the vehicle was a Tesla Model X, its aluminum shell clad in a matte-silver wrap, its roof adorned with a lighting rig and a modified rollbar to accommodate the gullwing doors. Said doors lifted and both Tauri and Typhoon stepped out. They turned into their dragon forms and approached Nicole.

"How are you feeling?" Typhoon asked.

"Been better," Nicole said. "Where's your Rolls? Couldn't make the climb?

Typhoon shook his head. "Bless its little heart. This type of environment is beyond its means. Besides, EVs are best for places like this, where ICE engines can generate enough carbon fumes to turn everyone into canaries."

"Makes sense," Nicole said.

"You can thank your brother for this little *donation*," Tauri said, gesturing to the car with his tail. "Echo salvaged it before the feds could take it away. I'm sure he wouldn't mind the little modifications we've made."

"Yeah, that looks like something Lucca would drive," Nicole said. "Anything to stroke his ego."

Typhoon turned to his two goons. "Unchain her, but keep her collar on for the time being."

"Oh, come on," Tokarev protested. "We spent forever trying to find chains to put on her."

"Then how is she supposed to walk?" Typhoon asked. "Unless you want to carry her."

Tokarev sighed and pressed a button on his remote. At once, the cuffs around her wings, wrists, and ankles unlatched. Nicole stretched her legs, felt her joints pop, and staggered to her feet. Her legs and spine were stiff, and there was a stabbing pain in her neck that kept her from moving it too much. This was made worse by the pain in her abdomen, which still hurt whenever she tried to move or take a deep breath. The more she thought of it, the more she wished she had stayed with Ito and the others, rather than go on this crazy, stupid recon mission.

Typhoon turned to Nikolai. "Have the other yokai been neutralized?"

"As far as we can tell," Nikolai said. "Our men have been scouring the caves for weeks, picking off any and all yokai we can find."

"Good," Typhoon said. "Then we shouldn't have too many issues. Let us proceed."

The Tesla led the way, illuminating the passage with its headlights, while the rest of them followed. Nicole could feel her ears pop and was overcome by a sinking feeling tightening her chest. They were walking into a trap, and no one was the wiser.

"You know it's not going to listen to you," Nicole said. "Or anyone, for that matter. It wants us to free it so it can destroy all those who defy it."

"Nonsense," Typhoon said. "It wants you, and I intend to grant it that wish."

"But it's tricking you," Nicole pleaded. "The myth of its birth was all a fib created by the Orochi to trick someone into freeing it."

Typhoon stopped and pulled Nicole aside. He gripped her shoulders and peered down at her with eyes of budding malice. "Nobody tricks me, child! Nobody, especially something that *I* created. *I* gave it life. *I* gave it the ability to think and feel. *I* gave it the objective to destroy my sister's creation and everything and everyone in it, and it *will* follow my every word until its dying breath!"

He shoved Nicole away, leaving deep imprints on her shoulders, and continued down the passage. Nicole grasped her shoulders and felt a strange coolness come over her. An icy chill that seemed to overpower the natural cold of the cave. She continued forward, taking up the rear, dreading whatever lay ahead at the end of their voyage.

Nicole saw light up at the end of the tunnel, and as they approached, she realized it was made by an array of spotlights that were all focused on a pair of stone doors. The doors had a jade orb in the center, like a giant green eye glowing under the shrill lighting. At the foot of a flight of stairs leading to the doors, and behind a pile of sandbags, soldiers gathered with their guns drawn. When they approached, the soldiers snapped to attention, which Typhoon acknowledged with a nod. The Tesla pulled off to the side as Nicole and the rest of the group reached the bottom of the stairs and stopped.

"Up there," Typhoon said, pointing to the doors, "is the chamber containing the egg of the Yamata no Orochi. You must place your hand on that orb to unlock it."

"Okay, but what's with all the protection?" Nicole asked.

"In case there are any other yokai behind the doors," Typhoon said.

"Lovely," Nicole said. She looked up at the stairs, her heart racing as she stared at the milky-green orb staring back at her.

"Well," Tauri said. "What are you waiting for? It's not going to touch itself."

"You wish," Nicole said as she climbed the steps. She realized halfway up that none of the others were following her, while the soldiers posted at the base all had their rifles trained on the doors. Nicole felt like a piece of bait and knew that she would be the first to suffer the brutality of whatever was waiting on the other side. She accepted her fate and continued up the stairs.

When she reached the doors, she stopped and said a small prayer to Blizzard for good luck. She closed her eyes and touched the orb. At first nothing happened, prompting Nicole to open one eye and check to see if anything had occurred. When the doors refused to budge, Nicole looked behind her.

"Now what?" she asked.

Typhoon opened his mouth to say something but was cut off by a sudden rumble. Nicole looked back at the doors to see them parting, slowly but surely, dumping a smattering of dust that rained down upon the steps below. Nicole lifted her hand from the jade ball and stepped back as the two doors parted, leaving the ball suspended at the top of a stone monolith that remained stoic as a wave of stale air swept over her. Nicole crouched down behind the steps, waiting for something, anything, to come out and take a swipe at her. But as her eyes watered under the bombardment of thousand-year-old air, nothing came out. No oni came out to attack her, and no flames burst from the pit of darkness beyond the threshold.

Nicole peaked up from behind the steps right as someone from behind shined one of the large spotlights into the chamber. In the light of the beam, Nicole saw a stony cavern, its floor and ceiling covered in stalactites and stalagmites, its rocky surface coated in a thin layer of moisture. At first, Nicole could not see anything out of the ordinary. But as the spotlight panned back and forth across the chamber, she noticed a large, round shape situated atop a stony pedestal. It was a large egg, roughly the size of a pickup truck, covered in green scales that reflected the light in bright twinkles. It sat atop a large stone altar that had been cut into the surrounding rock, which was flanked by a pair of dragon statues with rubies set into the eyes. Nicole sank her talons into the crevices of the stone as she took in the sight with trepidation. She rose to her feet and was met by Tauri and Typhoon.

"It's gorgeous," Tauri said.

"Indeed," Typhoon said. He stepped forward and the rest of the battalion followed. Even the Tesla managed to ascend the steps, its thick tires making mincemeat out of the stone. Nicole followed anxiously, as Tokarev reached through one of the passenger windows and took out an object that he handed to Typhoon. Typhoon grasped the object, which grew in size until it was almost twice the size of its original self, and Nicole saw it was a katana, clad in a black, wooden scabbard.

"This," Typhoon began, "is the Kusanagi no Tsurugi, the sword that was delivered from the neck of the eighth head of the original Orochi during its duel with Susanoo. Our men stole it from the Atsuta Shrine just yesterday and delivered it here so it might be used to scare the Orochi into submission." Typhoon handed the sword to Nicole. "The Orochi responds best to fear and intimidation. Having this at your side will convince it that you are its master, thus making it trust you more."

Nicole backed away from the sword. "I'm not taking that sword. I refuse to do anything else for you or for this foolish escapade of yours. It's clear that the Orochi wants me to free it so it can cause chaos and bloodshed wherever it goes, and I refuse to participate any longer."

Typhoon narrowed his eyes on Nicole. "You don't know how easily I can make your life a living hell, how I can make you suffer. I can make your life a walking nightmare, filled with the kind of pain and horror you only thought existed in the darkest confines of your mind."

"Fine then," Nicole said. "Kill me if you have to, but if you think for a second that I'm going to help you destroy the world and everyone in it, then you're not as smart as you think you are."

Typhoon turned towards Tokarev, who nodded and made his way to the back of the car.

"Perhaps a bit of prodding is needed," Typhoon said.

Nicole watched as Tokarev opened the hatchback and reached for something. He struggled for a bit, swearing in Russian as he fought for control of whatever was inside. Finally, he punched whoever it was in frustration and pulled them out, throwing them to the floor of the cave with a thud.

It was Nathan.

Nicole gasped. Nathan was wearing nothing but his boxers, his body covered in small cuts and bruises, and his hair a tangled mess matted with blood and sweat. A piece of duct tape was stretched over his mouth and his arms and feet were bound with zip ties. Tokarev ripped the tape off of Nathan's mouth and yanked out the dirty sock that had been crammed down his throat.

"Nicole," Nathan said, dryly.

"Nathan," Nicole screamed. She tried to approach, but Tauri held her back. "Nathan, what happened to you?"

"We intercepted him on his way home from the airport,"

Typhoon said. "He put up a fight, but our men managed to subdue him long enough to put him on a flight to Japan."

Tokarev took out his pistol and aimed it at the back of Nathan's skull.

"Don't do it," Nathan said. "Tell them to go to hell, Nicole, tell them-"

Tokarev pistol whipped Nathan, and he fell forward. Nicole struggled to run to his side, but Tauri held her firm.

"I want you to live, you know," Tauri whispered. "Before Lucio selected your brother to be your bride, I was considered a possible suitor. I've always dreamed of the day that I'd have you all to myself and make you my wife. Maybe, if you spend more time with us, you'll find I can give you more than whatever *he* can."

"I'll never be with someone who joins forces with a man who killed his family."

Tauri laughed. "Don't be silly, Nicole. It was *I* who burned them, not your father."

The dread Nicole felt earlier turned to numb and she felt herself loose wherever hope she still had. She felt Typhoon place the sword into her hands, felt his breath on her neck.

"Go on," Typhoon said. "Crack the egg."

"No," Nathan gasped.

But Nicole, sapped of her will, walked forward. She placed her hand upon the shell, felt its smooth, scaly surface, and felt something else press against the inside. She saw the egg shift ever so slightly, and then, the shell began to glow with vibrant luminescence. Nicole's heart thumped inside her chest, her tongue became dry, and every limb on her body shook. She glanced one last time at the group behind her, saw Tokarev with his pistol trained on Nathan's skull.

She turned back to the egg. This was it: she and Nathan were going to die, and the earth would die with them. She would be the cause of the apocalypse, and billions would suffer because of her.

But then, she recalled what Ito had said about the sword,

how it could kill the Orochi. She squeezed the scabbard in her hand, and a cold, hard reality washed over her. She would stab the egg, then stab herself. At the very least, she would die before hearing the shot ring out and know that the love of her life was gone from this world.

"Forgive me, Blizzard," Nicole whispered.

She shut her eyes and turned her head up, her nose pointed at the ceiling.

"Nathan, I love you."

She pulled the sword out of its scabbard.

"No!" Typhoon screamed.

"What the hell are you thinking?!" Tauri shouted.

"Tokarev, do something!" Nikolai said.

"*Der'mo*," Tokarev grumbled, his vest rattling as he fumbled for the remote. "*Sukin syn.*"

Nicole turned the blade towards the egg, and with all her might, plunged it though the shell.

CHAPTER 14

Nicole was blinded through her eyelids. A white flash enveloped her vision and waves of heat radiated over her. She was thrown back and landed on something large and metallic. All around her, chaos ensued. Gunshots rang out from every direction, and everyone was shouting. She lifted her head, felt shards of glass fall from her scales, and opened her eyes. In front of her, Nathan crouched in his dragon form, scorching a group of soldiers. On her left and right, guards ran this way and that, firing at anything that moved, while the sounds of dragons clawing and snapping at one another echoed off the stony walls.

And in front of her, the egg lay with a large, gaping hole, a pillar of green smoke spilling from its shell.

Nicole used the sword to prop herself up and realized she had fallen on top of the Tesla, its metal shell crushed under her weight like a tin can. She pulled herself up and ripped the collar off her neck. She looked for Nathan, and saw him standing over Tokarev, who was cowering beneath him like a scared animal. Tokarev emptied the pistol's magazine into Nathan's face, the bullets bouncing harmlessly against his scales, before tossing it aside.

"Please . . ." Tokarev begged. "I'll give you anything you want. Tell me the amount, and I'll write you the check. Please!"

But Nathan was not having it. He exhaled a small flame,

igniting Tokarev's clothes, leaving him to writhe and scream as the ammunition in his pockets went off and tore him to shreds.

Nathan turned to face her. "Are you okay?" he asked.

"Look who's talking," Nicole said. "What happened?"

"I puked on his shoes," Nathan said. "So he stripped me down to my boxers and sprayed me with freezing cold water." He turned and gestured to the mouth of the cave. "Friends of yours?"

Nicole looked to see a dozen or so serpentine dragons engaging with the soldiers from Echo and their dragon compatriots.

"It's the Hiroshima Satellite!" she said excitedly. "They've come to save us!"

"The who?" Nathan asked.

Before he could respond, Nicole detected movement from her left and turned just as Tauri charged at her. She moved out of the way swinging the sword and catching him just above his shoulder. Tauri grasped his wound and snarled.

"Hand over the Kusanagi," Tauri snarled

"Sure," Nicole said. "Bend over."

Tauri lunged at Nicole, his mouth wide, his talons flashing. Nicole sprinted to meet him, the blade pointed towards his stomach, but he knocked it out of the way with his talons and attempted to wrench the blade from her. He shoved her backwards, forcing her onto her back, his snapping jaws just inches from her face. She saw fire boil in his throat and turned away, but before Tauri could burn her, she heard him choke and wheeze. Nathan was on his back, his wrist-stinger embedded in Tauri's side. Blood and venom oozed from the point of entry, and his grip weakened. Nicole broke the sword free from Tauri, and knocked him in the teeth with the hilt, then kicked him away.

Nathan held out his hand, which Nicole took with grace.

"Thanks," she said. "I owe you one."

"Don't mention it," he said.

"Nicole!" Chyanne said. She sprinted towards her, arms wide, and they embraced. "Dear god, I thought I lost you."

"How did you find me?" Nicole said, straining as her mother squeezed the stuffing out of her.

Chyanne let go. "The sanctum found me after we didn't come back from our excursion. Ito used his oni friends to find you by tracking your scent, before Daisuke called for reinforcements from Tokyo."

Sure enough, in addition to dragons, there were also red oni, their clubs swinging wildly at anything that dared challenge them. But amidst all the violence, one force reigned supreme above all. In the center of the chamber, Typhoon stood, burning dragon and oni alike with his fire. His eyes shimmered and his teeth glowed red as flames poured from his mouth. On the other side of the cave, Seth and Daisuke hunched down and returned fire from behind a rock, but their flames did little to phase Typhoon.

Behind them, a loud crack echoed through the cave like a clap of thunder. Nicole looked to see seven new holes form in the side of the egg next to the one she had made. Columns of green smoke rose from the shattered shell, their forms taking on long, almost serpentine shapes.

"We've gotta get out of here," Nicole said. "That thing's going to hatch any minute and it's going to take the whole cave with it."

A tumble of rocks fell from the ceiling and Nicole leapt out of the way. She looked up to see the egg pulsating light, and with a thunderous crack of sparks, the top of the shell blew open. Columns of smoke rose higher in the chamber, and the more Nicole looked, the more it seemed the columns were forming into the shape of eight, long necks.

"Look," Nathan said, pointing up. Nicole did so and saw a small hole in the ceiling of the cave.

"Let's go!" Nicole said. She flapped her wings, and the others followed. She flew as fast as she could, hoping to escape the chaos below. She looked back and saw Nathan, her mother, and the other friendly dragons following her lead. Seth and Daisuke took up the rear, their wings flapping rapidly. But before they could get any higher, Typhoon lunged towards them, grabbing Seth by the ankle and pulling him down.

"Seth!" Nicole screamed. She abandoned her ascent and swooped back towards the floor of the cave. She reached them just as Typhoon was wrapping his talons around Seth's neck, his mouth starting to glow with a hideous red haze.

"Oh no you don't," Nicole said. She leapt onto Typhoon and thrusted the blade she was still holding into his mouth. Typhoon gagged and staggered backwards, as Nicole pulled the blade back and pointed it at him.

"Come any closer," she snarled, placing herself between him and Seth.

Typhoon coughed up a mouthful of blood and spit. "You've got a bigger problem here than me, kid."

"I hate to say it," Seth said, pulling himself up, "but I think he's right."

Nicole turned just in time to see the columns of smoke morph from gaseous fumes to a solid figure. Thick, green scales emerged, red eyes opened at the end of large heads, and teeth grew from formless masses to make eight threatening mouths that snapped and jeered at them.

The Orochi, unleashed from its confines, let out a hideous roar that erupted from the very bowels of hell.

Typhoon marched towards the creature and stood resolute. "Hear me, oh mighty one," he said. "For I am your master, and by law, you must"–

With a single swing from one of his heads, the Orochi knocked him out of the way, sending Typhoon flying into a nearby wall. The creature let out an even louder cry, causing the ground to heave beneath it.

"Let's get the hell out of here," Seth said. He leapt towards the opening and Nicole followed, resisting the urge to look back at the hideous creature that had been unleashed onto the world. Above her, the gash in the ceiling exposed a blue sky above that beckoned and called to her. She felt the air caress her face and the sun warm her scales, and she yearned to get out of this prison and never look back. She was almost there when she felt a stabbing pain in her ankle, and something pulling her backwards. Nicole looked down and saw Tauri grasping her. His teeth were damp with blood and his eyes red with madness.

"Please!" Tauri gasped. "Don't leave me!"

"Too late," Nicole said. She brought the tip of the blade down onto his face, cleaving his eye. He let go, while the heads of the Orochi rose up and moved towards him.

Nicole did not wait around to watch what happened next. She turned her eyes away and flapped even harder towards the light. But despite her best effort, nothing could save her ears from the sound. Tarui's screams of pain were drowned out only by the sounds of his flesh tearing and his bones breaking, a sickening symphony that made Nicole's stomach twist into knots. The thought of her being next propelled her faster than she had ever flown in her life, and finally, she escaped the confines of the cave and was free.

CHAPTER 15

When Nicole emerged from the mountain peak, the first thing she did was look for her friends. All around, serpentine dragons milled about the foothills, tending to their wounds and caring for the injured. Behind her, green smoke rose from the top of the mountain like a volcano, and out in the distance, sirens blared and emergency vehicles made their way up the foothills. Eventually, Nicole caught a glimpse of golden scales and spotted Nathan, her mother, Seth, and Daisuke near a bend in the Hii River. Nicole banked and descended towards them. When she landed, she stuck the blade of the sword into the dirt, then dashed over to hug Nathan. They embraced, and Nicole melted into Nathan's grasp as his wings covered her.

"I thought you were doomed," Nicole said. "I didn't think I could save you."

"You did great," Nathan said. "You saved us both."

She kissed him and coiled her tail with his, only letting go when she noticed her mother looking over Nathan's shoulder. She looked up and saw Chyanne was smiling at them.

"I wish I could have met you under different circumstances," Chyanne said.

Nathan regained his composure and held out his talon. "It's a pleasure to meet you, Ms. Newheart."

"Please," Chyanne said, taking it, "call me Chyanne."

Daisuke and Seth came up beside her.

"I'm glad you're in one piece," Daisuke said. "I was worried it was too late."

Nicole glanced over her shoulder at the mountain, which was spewing more of the inky, greenish-black smoke. "It is too late. The Orochi hatched, and it's only a matter of time before it breaks free."

Seth sauntered over to the sword and grasped it by the hilt. "At least you have that magical sword Ito was talking about."

"That's not the Kusanagi." Ito drifted down from the trees above and landed on Seth's shoulder. "That's Susanoo's old sword, the one he used to kill the original Orochi."

"But Typhoon said they stole it from the shrine in Nagoya," Nicole said.

"They must have got it mixed up," Ito said. "This is a Katana. The Kusanagi was a Tsurugi, an older, double-edged sword that predates the Katana by several centuries. It was also made of bone, not steel, and its hilt was fashioned from the neck vertebrae of the Orochi's eighth head. Besides," Ito pointed to the blade, "this one's been reforged. You can even see where it shattered when Susanoo decapitated the eighth head."

Nicole looked to where Ito pointed and observed a fine, hairlike crease along the side of the blade that would not have been visible to the untrained eye.

"Then where is the real sword?" Nicole asked.

"I can find out," Ito said. He whistled, and from the side of a nearby tree trunk, a creature emerged that confused and baffled Nicole at the same time. It had the body of a bear, the head of an elephant, and the tail of an ox, with blue fur, white tusks, and a golden mane.

"Listen, Baku," Ito said. "Find me the real Kusanagi, then tell me its location."

"*Kashikomarimashita,*" the Baku said, before lifting off the ground and hovering away into the sky.

Nathan rubbed his eyes and watched as the creature vanished over the horizon. "What the hell was that?"

"A Baku," Ito said. "It's a friendly yokai that feeds on bad dreams. The one I just talked to can also find things when they are lost or forgotten."

Nathan nodded, his eyes transfixed on Ito in a look of confusion. "Okay," Nathan said. "I'm going to pretend I understood everything you just said to me and hope I'm not still tripping on sedatives."

Nicole laughed. "It's fine, Nate. Ito's a friendly dragon, and he's here to help."

"I'm actually a Kami," Ito said, "but now's not the time to play semantics."

As they spoke, Nicole noticed the river had turned a shade of dark red. The substance clouded the stream and worked its way down the mountain, staining the shoreline and causing the fish within it to die and float to the surface. Around them, Nicole could hear screams of panic as other members of the sanctum took note of the Exodus-like plague that was unfolding before them.

"What the . . .?" Nicole asked. She was caught off guard by a sudden explosion of rock from the peak above, followed by a crash and the telltale screech of the Orochi. The eight heads of the creature burst from the top of the mountain, nearly twice as large as before, its eyes glowing red hot against its mossy scales. Its massive talons pulled it up and out of its confinement, and when the smoke cleared, Nicole could see streams of blood trickling down between its shoulders and its eight necks. A pair of wings grew from its back, tearing away the flesh and scales. The Orochi released a cry of pain as blood spilled down the side of the mountain, overflowing the rivers and rolling down the hills. Nicole and the others sprang up as a torrent of red nearly washed them away. Nicole almost felt sorry for the creature, forced to endure such pain so early. But then she saw its size, its magnitude, and realized the Orochi was bigger than anything she could have imagined. The wings stretched its membrane taut and the creature's screams turned into roars of fury. It flapped and lifted into the air, generating gusts of wind that nearly lifted Nicole and the others away. The creature turned and aimed north, flapping its wings and making the trees arc against the mighty gale in its wake. Nicole struggled to hold herself midair, and would have fallen out of the sky had Nathan not flown to her rescue, grabbing her by the shoulders and bracing her against the wind.

Nicole looked at him and smiled, but her smile faded when she saw the destruction left in the Orochi's wake. The landslide caused by the mountain had ravaged the town below: roofs of buildings were ripped off, bloody mud caked itself against every surface and villagers stood, stunned and horrified at the state of their bellowed town.

And then there was the Orochi itself, its shape growing smaller as it soared to an unknown destination.

Ito flew over to Nicole, his tiny wings flapping like those of a hummingbird. "I have the means of tracking him," he said. "I can call on the yokai to give me news of its movements."

"That's good," Nicole said. "But what about this?"

Ito looked down at the destruction and shook his head. "It is but a taste of what's to come now that the Orochi is reborn."

* * *

The rest of the day was spent cleaning up the devastation wrought by the Orochi's flyby. Much like how she had done in New York, Nicole assisted the Tokyo Sanctum in sifting through the rubble for survivors and digging through the thick grime of blood and dirt to allow rescue crews safe passage. Once everything was cleared and the survivors were sent to hospital, the villagers who remained organized a *kagura* in a nearby shrine. Daisuke explained it was a ritual dance within Shintoism intended to appease certain gods and spirits, and that the villagers wished to perform one in hopes of pleading out to friendly entities. As night fell, the priests and the villagers lit a bonfire near the shrine's gates, gathered large drums and flute, and prepared for the ancient and holy ritual. And in lieu of the dragon prop that had been damaged during the events of the day, Daisuke volunteered himself to take its place in the procession.

As Nicole watched Daisuke dance and strut around the fire to the beat of the drums and the whistle of the flute, she guessed this was not the first time he had participated in such a ritual. She was sitting at the front of the circle, Nathan to her right, Ito to her left, and her mother and Seth further along the edge of the procession. She watched the figures as they transformed into black silhouettes against yellow flames. She was hypnotized by the harmonious way in which they moved. She saw the urgency in their movements, heard their pleas in the music. She felt the villager's collected fear and longing for a miracle of some kind, a prayer for peace, and deliverance from evil.

Nicole turned to Ito, who was watching the Kagura intently.

"Now what?" she asked. The question had been on her tongue since the Orochi vanished over the horizon.

"We wait," Ito said. "Once we know where the Kusanagi rests, and find where the Orochi is located, we can devise a plan to defeat it."

Nathan arched his head over Nicole and glanced at Ito. "Do you know where the Orochi is right now?"

Ito shook his head. "None of the yokai or Kami in the land have told me they've seen it. The last I heard, it vanished north into the Sea of Japan. Where it will go from there is anyone's guess, though I'm thinking it'll probably come back once it heals from its wounds."

"Wait a minute," Nathan said. "How did they tell you when you were here with us all day?"

Ito tapped his temple. "Telepathy, my dear boy," he said. "I can hear the voices of all spirits who inhabit this land of ours."

Nicole sighed. The dynamics of this endeavor were becoming more complicated by the moment.

"How can we be sure it will come back?" Nathan asked.

"Where else will it go?" Ito said. "Japan is its home, or at least its adopted home. It knows this land more closely than any other locale. I would be shocked if it decided to attack another nation."

"If only I hadn't stabbed that damn egg," Nicole said. "We wouldn't be in this mess had I just waited."

"Be not ashamed, Nicole," Ito said. "You didn't know, and you attempted something truly noble. Besides, given its power and influence over mortals and immortals alike, the Orochi would have found a way to free itself eventually."

Nicole sank to her stomach, planting her jaw on top of her talons. She closed her eyes and recalled her final thought before stabbing the egg, and her intention. She felt so weak, so pitiful. She had contemplated suicide in the past, back when she was still a teenager reeling from her mother's 'death'. The thought of it hadn't occurred in years, and thinking about it now put her in the darkest of moods, the saddest of dispositions.

Then, as though he read her mind, Nathan placed a wing over her like a blanket. She leaned into the warmth of his yellow scales. Only his presence at a time like this could make her heart all warm and gooey inside.

Nicole's attention was captured by the Baku from earlier descending from the skies. The festivities grew silent as the creature landed at the edge of the bonfire and gestured to Ito, who eagerly hopped over to where it sat. The creature whispered something incomprehensible to Ito. Nicole strained herself to hear anything, in the remote possibility that they weren't speaking Japanese. But all she heard were muffled words accompanied by a sea of different expressions on Ito's face that could've passed for the seven stages of grief in condensed form. But then his eyes widened, he whispered back a nervous question, and recoiled at what the Baku said. Finally, when the Baku was done, Ito thanked it and stepped back to address the crowd.

"According to the Baku," Ito said, "the Kusanagi is buried in a cave at the foot of Mount Fuji, deep within the forests of

Aokigahara."

There was a gasp through the crowd. Even Daisuke seemed taken aback, his former composure shattered by this revelation. But Nicole felt like she was missing something. What was so horrible about this one forest at the foot of the most famous volcano on earth?

"Um . . ." Nathan said. "Isn't that the suicide forest?"

"Unfortunately, yes," Ito said, solemnly. "For centuries, people who were in pain have traveled to the forest to take their lives. Today, it is haunted by *yurei*, or the spirits of those who died there and were never given a proper burial. What's worse, I have no power over them; I cannot control human spirits, and if we go there seeking the Kusanagi, we will be putting ourselves at considerable risk."

"What kind of risk?" Nicole asked.

"They can consume your very soul," Ito said. "The yurei who live there are in constant pain . . . and are all too eager to spread that pain wherever they go. Aokigahara is full of them. It's a place of darkness, and any venture there will be extremely dangerous."

Nicole felt her stomach twist into knots. She never believed in ghosts, but she would be the first to admit that ghost stories and horror movies scared her stiff. As such, the thought of venturing into such a place, a place teeming with angry, vengeful spirits, made her shrink deeper into the folds of Nathan's wings.

There was a crash behind them, and Nicole nearly leapt out of her scales. Everyone turned, and Nicole spotted a black dragon covered with dried blood staggering towards the bonfire like a drunkard. He stopped by the light of the fire and propped himself against the side of the archway. It took Nicole a moment to realize it was Typhoon, but when she did, she sprang to her feet and spread her wings to protect Nathan.

"Fear not," Typhoon said. "I'm sorry to interrupt anyone's . . . festivities. It just took me half the day to dig myself out of the muck sprung from the Orochi's scales." Typhoon coughed and a red cloud burst from his mouth. "Rarely . . . do I . . . admit my fault but today is one of them. I thought I could control the monster I created centuries ago. I ignored the warning signs, thinking it would at least listen to its creator, that it could be controlled. But I was wrong."

"Why did you create that abomination?" Nicole spat.

"To help me fight my sister," Typhoon said. "Millions of years ago, before weredragons were even a flicker in a mind's eye, I sparred with my sister, Blizzard. I created the Orochi to assist me, to fight her children and thin her forces. But she bested it, and in its final moment of anguish it cursed me and never forgave the motive behind its creation. And now, having unleashed it, I am powerless to stop it." He glanced up at Nicole. "You need not blame yourself, Nicole. You may have broken the egg, but I was the impetus behind today's events. You were merely the tool, and I was the flash in the pan."

"Thank you for relinquishing me from my sins," Nicole said. "But how does that get us anywhere closer to defeating this thing?"

"It doesn't," Typhoon said. "But I can give you some advice. When you engage with it, Hachi will attempt to drag you down to the deepest depths of despair. You must resist his advances, lest you suffer and let him win. And if there is one thing I want more than anything right now, it's for that monster to lose."

"Hachi?" Nathan asked.

"The eighth head," Typhoon said. "Where the intelligence is kept. Soon it will attempt to absorb all knowledge in its vicinity to get a drop on its prey."

As Typhoon spoke, Nicole noticed the villagers reach for their phones, the screens of which were white with static and emitting a screeching noise that reminded her of an emergency alert. Beyond the gates, the night air filled with the jumbled and static squeal of a hundred or so car radios, flipping though stations as though their dials had minds of their own. Throughout the village, telephones rang off the hook and TVs played at max volume, while a symphony of computer error messages usurped the ambient noise of the night. Nicole's heart sank; even though he was visible, she could sense the Orochi's presence and feel its breath on the wind."

"There it goes," Typhoon said. "That's what I designed it to do, to learn as much as it can in a short period of time, so that I wouldn't have to waste time teaching and training it."

"So why don't you kill it yourself?" Seth asked.

"Because I don't have the damned sword," Typhoon said. "The Kusanagi was an insurance policy in case I needed to start from scratch, but it's been so long since I laid eyes on it that I forgot what it looked like." Typhoon scoffed. "I had my men carry out a raid on a shrine all for nothing."

"Then how do you expect us to defeat it?" Nicole asked.

"Use your brain, child," Typhoon said. "Venture into the Sea of Trees and liberate the Kusanagi from its hiding spot. As for me, earth is no longer a viable habitat. I've tried for years to reclaim this place after my sister abandoned it, but things have moved too fast." He turned and spread his wings, shaking off flecks of dried blood as he did. "I must go now, to other places that are worth my time. I may not be able to undermine my sister here but elsewhere is fair game." He flapped his wings, nearly blowing out the fire, and hovered.

"And if you manage to best it," Typhoon said, "make sure the Kusanagi enters the heart. That's where its soul is kept."

Typhoon turned and flapped, rising higher into the sky, until he vanished into the night.

CHAPTER 16

Hachi gazed upon the sea of clouds before them, hours after he and his brothers emerged from the egg. Thick, puffy forms blanketed a dark sky set with stars and the large, looming vestige of the moon covered everything with bluish-white light. As Hachi bathed in the cool lunar glow, the horns on his head grew hot. Knowledge entered the horns, drawn to them like moths to a flame, opening Hachi's mind to the strange new world that greeted him. Names, places, events, people, and dragons.

"Incredible," Hachi said. "Such wonder. Such progress."

The other heads looked up at him, mute and curious, like dogs looking towards their master. He heard their thoughts, words inside the confines of his skull.

Hungry, feed, hungry.

"Yes, my brothers," Hachi said. "We must eat before we can continue with our plan."

Plan?

"Why else were we born?" Hachi asked. "Why else did Typhoon create us? To kill, to destroy. But lo, he too betrayed us in the end, fled this world while Blizzard and her minions tore us to shreds and left us for dead, banishing us to a state of birth and rebirth." Hach grit his teeth. "We do not heed his call now. We are our own legion, and we will destroy what he created, too."

Legion, destroy.

The fourth head, Yon, snapped his jaws, strings of saliva dripping from between his fangs.

"Patience, Yon," Hachi said with a smile. "We must ensure our time of glory is not wasted."

The heads nodded and purred in approval, except for Ichi, the first head, who noticed something behind them. Hachi followed his gaze and saw a large, winged beast approaching them from behind.

"Ah," Hachi said. "A magic flying craft. The humans created those because they wished to dominate the air as they did the land and sea."

Blasphemy, heresy, hunger.

"But we'll show them who's the Emperor up here."

The Orochi faced the approaching craft. Hachi salivated at the thought of the humans inside, their screams, their calls for help. The craft dived, but the Orochi was faster. Hachi felt his talons wrap around the middle of the craft and tighten, the metal tearing beneath their claws. They brought it up, and Hachi watched as his brothers bit into the metal hull and ripped it open. The vacuum sucked several screaming humans out to their deaths. Hachi caught one in his mouth and bit down. The tiny bones crunched between his jaws and his mouth filled with delectable juices he hadn't tasted in over seven centuries.

He glanced down; passengers remained strapped in, their belts rigid. A smile graced Hachi's face. He and his brothers dined on the passengers, ripping them out of their seats and eating them like grapes from a vine. Some fought back, punching and kicking Hachi's lips and jaws, but it only made the thrill of the hunt all the more enjoyable. Hachi and his brothers spared no one; men, women, young and old alike all ended up in the large stomach they shared.

When Hachi and his siblings were finished, they dropped the craft and watched it plummet, its shape growing smaller as it fell to earth.

Ichi growled to get Hachi's attention. He turned to see his brother offering something in his mouth: it was a human in fancy dress, the mage who piloted this magical craft using his little hat to viciously beat Ichi on the nose.

"Dear brother," Hachi said. "Your dedication to our cause touches me so. Yet, I wish to save room for what's next. Have him for yourself, dear brother. Enjoy this moment of victory."

Ichi nodded and swallowed the human in a single gulp.

Humbled, grateful.

"Now," Hachi said, "onwards, to Naniwa-kyo."

❊ ❊ ❊

They broke through the clouds and descended towards the city that glimmered in the night. Naniwa-kyo was lit by magical lights that turned night to day, from towers that could almost touch the stars.

"Impressive," Hachi said. "The humans have captured the stars and use them to light their cities."

Colorful, bright.

Hachi could smell the humans walking along the canals, their faces stuffed with sweet food and bountiful drink. Hachi's mouth watered; he could not wait to sink his teeth into the savory humans, their bodies made succulent by the fatty food they dined upon.

Canal?

"Yes, I don't remember the canal either. Must be a new feature they added when we were in limbo."

Spotted.

"Good," Hachi replied.

They lowered their trajectory and flew with the canal to their chest. Beneath them, humans screamed and ran for their lives, pouring out of their horseless carriages and taking shelter wherever they could. The Orochi swooped down, and Hachi and his brothers began their second feast of the night, consuming anyone they could get their teeth on. Hachi heard the crack of iron cannons, but he felt nothing as the bolts bounced harmlessly off their scales.

They flew until Hachi spotted the green, sloping roofs of a castle nestled amid the towers. Curious, they flew towards it, circled, and landed gently within the castle's large moat.

"This is new," Hachi said. "When did they build this? And why didn't they make it as tall as the other structures?"

Knowledge?

"It comes to me gradually, brothers," Hachi said. "For all I know, this place isn't called Naniwa-kyo anymore."

Osaka.

"How do you know that?"

Inscriptions.

"And how on earth can you read? I should be the one reading the inscriptions to you."

Knowledge.

"Whatever. Just shut up and help me raise this thing. It probably has magical properties we can use for our cause."

The ground began to shake as something very large approached from above. Hachi looked up, and saw a dark shape with a pair of black wings.

"Typhoon!" Hachi cried. "Oh, how I longed to give you a piece of my mind. Speak to me, now that I've regained my memory, and–"

Bomb! Fire! Dead!

A wave of pain engulfed Hachi and they fell onto the castle, shattering its walls and collapsing its roof. Blood poured from his mouth and those of his brothers, turning the moat red. He felt their flesh exposed, the scales burned away by the fiery energy they had endured, as the world began to blur and twist.

And then he saw her, the maiden of white and blue, a creature so pure that she made his insides turn to honey. He had known her before he hatched, beckoned her, called her to free him, and she did free him. This merciful maiden had given him another chance to live, to spread his wings, to feel the sun on his scales after centuries in darkness.

And he wanted her more than ever.

Nicole.

Hachi closed his eyes and focused his energy on the skies above. He felt his scales warm and the inside of his eyelids filled with light. He opened them and saw their scales were glowing green like a jade effigy. Above, the black shape returned to finish them off. His brothers ducked, their heads and necks twisting among one another in an embrace, but Hachi stood firm. He knew what was coming, and he knew he could defeat it with their last line of defense.

Heart. Bleed.

There was a thunderous crack, and violent shockwaves emanated from the Orochi's heart. Hachi opened his eyes to see the shape fall out of the sky and buildings crumble to dust. The city grew dark as an invisible force chased away all light, and when it was all over, Naniwa-kyo was covered by a veil of darkness. There were no screams, nor firing of cannons. The city was dead, except for the sound of rubble crashing in the distance.

Hachi forced the rest of his brothers up and surveyed the gray wasteland they had created.

Power, power, destruction.

"Yes, brothers," Hachi said. "We are more powerful than any being, but we must never let ourselves falter, lest we be bested by human magic."

Heal, wounds, hurt, bleeding.

"Lick the wounds," Hachi said. "Heal our damaged scales. As for me, I must contact the maiden who saved us, learn where she is, and repay her for her service to our cause."

Hachi's brothers proceeded to lick the wounds on their back, letting their saliva harden their flesh and rid it of pain, while Hachi's eyes rolled into the back of his head, and his mind reached like telepathic tendrils to the bright and beautiful Nicole.

"Where are you, my queen?" Hachi said. "Speak to me. Hear me. Tell me where you are, or where you're going, and I'll come to you. Just show me…"

CHAPTER 17

Nicole woke with a jolt when the light bulb in the lamp by her bed exploded in a shower of sparks. Scrambling to her feet, she nearly knocked over the privacy screen as she untangled herself from the blankets. She stood in the room for a moment, unmoving, watching the smoke rise from the top of the lamp. Absent-mindedly, Nicole adjusted the straps of her tank top and wondered if it was a waking dream. But elsewhere in the house, she heard commotion and realized something was wrong. Dazed and half asleep, she staggered towards the nightstand, careful not to slip on the feet of her pajama pants, and reached for her phone to see what time it was. But the phone was dead, its buttons unresponsive, its screen black as the night outside. She grabbed its charger and tried to plug it in, but the phone remained bricked.

"Nicole?" Nathan said. He was standing in the doorway, dressed in a black *yukata*, or a type of kimono used as sleep wear.

"You're having the same issues?" Nicole asked.

Nathan nodded. "The power went out."

"It's not just the house," Daisuke said, appearing in the doorway behind Nathan. "The whole village lost power. Not even the landlines work."

Seth appeared next to Daisuke, rubbing his eyes and yawning. "Just when I thought I could shake my jetlag."

From beyond the doors leading to the courtyard, Nicole could hear villagers talking amongst themselves in panicked chatter. She heard car doors slam, but no engines started, and it dawned on her that the ambient sound of cars, trains, or airplanes had ceased.

There was a patter of feet from the other side of the sliding door, and the outline of a small creature appeared opposite the rice paper. Nicole sprinted to the door and slid it open. Ito hurried inside and collapsed by the foot of her bed. He was panting, and his wings hung lazily at his side like he had flown the length of the country. He lifted his head, his tiny tongue dangling from the side of his jaw.

"What's wrong?" Nicole asked.

"Everything," Ito said. "The Orochi touched down in Osaka. He decimated the city, then created something akin to an electromagnetic pulse that took down the power grid for the entire Japanese mainland." He paused to catch his breath.

"This is the Orochi's fault?" Nicole asked, gesturing around.

Ito nodded. "It was part of his final defense, called the heartbleed. It's triggered when he's injured and needs space to heal, and in this instance, it decimated all of Osaka."

Ito buried his head in the blankets by the edge of Nicole's bed, and his wings wilted like dying flower petals.

Nicole looked back at the others in the doorway.

"I guess I have no choice then," she said. "I have to go to the Sea of Trees and find the Kusanagi."

"We'll come with you," Daisuke said.

Nicole held up her hand. "No," she replied. "I only want one person to come with me."

Her eyes turned to Nathan.

"J . . . just me?" he asked.

"Yes," Nicole said. "And Ito." She approached Nathan and put her hands on his shoulders. "If anything happens to me, I need you to carry the sword in my stead."

"But shouldn't we have more support?" Nathan asked. "Perhaps from someone older and more experienced?"

"I don't think anyone is experienced enough for this," Nicole said. "Besides, we need dragons here we can trust to hold the fort while we're away."

"Honey," Chyanne said, "I think Nathan's right."

Nicole looked and saw her mother sitting up in bed.

"Mom," she said. "This is—"

"Stupid," Chyanne said, "that's what it is. Have someone more experienced go. Have them deal with the damn Orochi. You've done enough."

"With all due respect," Ito said, his face still partially buried in the blanket, "the sword prefers your daughter to wield it in battle. Anyone can take its hilt, but in the hands of Nicole, it'll be a completely different weapon." He looked up. "Trust me, I can sense what the sword thinks and feels as though it were a living being."

Chyanne turned away to stare into the shadows. She shook her head.

"This is too much," she said. "I unlocked a Pandora's box by landing in Okinawa. God, I'm so stupid." She buried her face in her hands. "Stupid girl, stupid, stupid . . ."

Nicole dashed over to her mother's side and knelt beside her.

"Do you believe in fate?" Nicole asked.

Chyanne shook her head.

"I do," Nicole said. "I believe I was meant to find Nathan to help him along when he turned for the first time. I believe it was fate that brought him and I together, so that dad could be defeated, and our kind could be liberated. And I believe I was brought here to defeat the Orochi, and prevent it from wreaking chaos upon the world, so that future generations can't arouse its wrath."

Chyanne looked at Nicole, her face haggard, her eyes bloodshot.

"You believe in all that jargon?"

"Considering all that's happened to us," Nicole said, "I think Blizzard's had a guiding hand in everything we've done up until this point."

Chyanne stared gloomily into the darkness.

"When do you need to leave?" she asked, defeated.

"The sooner the better," Ito said. "I think if we leave at sunrise, we can reach Mount Fuji by nightfall."

Chyanne glanced over her shoulder at Nathan.

"Look after her for me, okay?" she said. Chyanne rolled onto her side, pulled the covers up to her neck, and shut her eyes.

Nicole was tempted to wake her, but Nathan took her hand.

"We'll do this together, okay," he said. "You and me."

Nicole nodded and took his hand in hers.

"Together," she repeated, and kissed him.

CHAPTER 18

The trio left at dawn. Heading north, Nicole watched Japan come to life with the beginning of a new day, but as she had expected, there were no cars and trains. Indeed, there were few signs of modernity to be spotted. A derailed train, a pileup on a highway, and a burnt-out substation were reminders that life had abruptly reverted to an older time, with little regard for modern sensibilities. Nicole flew in silence, her mother's words stinging her eyes and conjuring tears, which in turn were picked up by the wind and flung behind her head.

"Why do you cry?" Ito asked. The little Kami clung to her neck; his small wings were too light to carry him far.

"She's never going to talk to me again," Nicole said. "My mother . . . she's spent years wanting to see me again, and I abandoned her."

"You didn't abandon her," Nathan said, coming up on her side. "You said what you were going to do and meant it. It doesn't mean goodbye forever."

Nicole looked back at him and blinked away tears. "Does she think that? So many dragons have left her in her life. Now I'm leaving her for the second time." She sniffed, trying hard to swallow her tears. "Why does this have to be *my* destiny? Why can't it be a member of the Tokyo Sanctum, or someone else?"

Ito leaned forward and nuzzled her with his nose. "Have you ever considered your birth to be of special importance?"

"My father did," Nicole said, "but he knew nothing. He had his plans and wanted to use me for ill intentions."

"Well," Ito said, "maybe he was wrong. Maybe he thought poorly. Maybe your birthdate means something more than he could have imagined."

Nicole thought for a moment, her dried tears cracking against the sides of her face. "I was the first weredragon born in the twenty-first century. My birth came with the passing of a new millennium, and since my birth on the stroke of midnight, in the year 2000, my heart has beat a total of seven-hundred thousand times. But it's just a day, at least, that's what I've always thought."

"But you've got to admit," Ito said, "you have wondered, no?"

Nicole could not deny it. Even during her darkest days, when she cursed the words of her father like it was bile in her mouth, she had wondered: *does my life mean anything?*

"Baby," Nathan said, "if I can add anything, I would say that before I met you, I didn't think there was anything left to find out about me, about this world. But in the last few months, I've learned more about myself than I could ever hope to, and I'll probably keep learning until the day I die. Maybe there's more to learn about you."

"Maybe . . ." Nicole trailed off. She felt uneasy as if she knew she was about to uncover something ugly that would affect her for the rest of her life. She pondered for a moment and wondered if, perhaps, there was something to her father's superstitions, to everyone's opinions about her and her existence.

"We're going to fly over the remains of Osaka in an hour or two," Ito said. "I advise we go around, as the military presence in the area is pretty intense at the moment."

"Is the Orochi still there?" Nathan asked.

Suddenly, a pair of jets flew overhead, the force of the wind nearly knocking them off kelter.

"I think it's disappeared again," Ito said. "My Yokai friends told me that it departed north not long ago."

"That's where we're headed," Nathan said.

"Maybe he's trying to get to the sword before we do," Nicole said.

"Then we better hurry," Ito said. "Do either of you need a rest?"

"No," Nicole said, flapping harder. "I won't sleep until I have that sword."

* * *

Hours later, the trio landed on the edge of Aokigahara forest. Mt. Fuji loomed overhead, its snow-capped peak shimmering in the receding light. Above them, gray clouds rolled in, and Nicole could smell rain on the night air. In front of her, the sunlight seemed to fade faster as the thick labyrinth of trees stretched out before them. Twisted and gnarled branches blotted out the light from above to create a canopy of darkness. She could see why it was called the Sea of Trees, for it felt to her less like a forest and more like a wild and untamed ocean.

Nicole felt her scales tremble as she stared into its depths, and felt something stare back.

"So, now what?" Nathan asked.

"We go by foot," Ito said. "Flying is far too dangerous, especially in such thick foliage."

"Why can't we fly above it?" Nicole said.

"It'll be harder to find what we're looking for," Ito said. He licked his finger and held it up. "What we are looking for is underground, and if my instincts are correct, we should go this way." Ito pointed to a path that traversed towards the left. Beyond, the shadows of Aokigahara were thickening as raindrops pelted the leaves and a distant rumble of thunder sounded from some ways away.

Nicole felt herself edging towards Nathan, who leaned into her in response. Even though she knew little of this forest, what few mentions were made of it were enough to give her pause.

Suicide. Death. Hungry spirits. The yurei. Despite the size of her dragon form, their presence made her feel small and weak.

The trees rustled in the breeze and Nicole thought she heard someone moan far off in the distance. She couldn't place it, but to her, it sounded like a cry of pain.

"The yurei know we're here," Ito said. "But we haven't a choice to avoid them." He stepped forward onto the path and turned back. "Please, stay close."

Nicole and Nathan followed him through the canopy of trees. Inside the forest, there was no sound, only a deathly silence that was occasionally interrupted by the rustle of branches or the falling rain. The air was thick and cold, and the ground beneath her seeped with mud between her talons. All around, behind the trees and rocks and tangle of branches, she felt cold eyes staring at her, tracking her, sizing her up. A chill ran down her back into her tail, and her scales began to tremble. Every sound was a demon or something horrible that sought to eat her soul, and the forest itself felt like it was trying to consume her.

"This is fine," Nicole lied to herself. "It's just a forest, a very creepy forest where people go to take their lives sometimes. There's nothing special about it."

"Hey look," Nathan said, gesturing to something on his left. Nicole peered at what appeared to be a length of yellow ribbon, tied between two trees. "I've read about these," Nathan continued. "Hikers use these to retrace their steps if they ever get lost."

"We can use it to help us find our way back," Ito said. "But let's not get distracted."

Nicole lingered behind as the others continued on, staring at the ribbon. Could it be, rather than a way for people to find their way out, it was a signal to others that their remains were nearby? Did this person ever find their way out of this hellish place? Nicole tried to suppress the thoughts in her mind and caught up with the others, leaving the ribbon to the mercy of the forest.

They continued onward, until they reached a notch in the path that veered to the right. Ito paused, stuck his finger out, and ventured to the left, into the thicket.

"Ito, that's not the path," Nicole said.

"I'm aware of that," he said. "What we seek is not on any path. Come. Follow me."

It was easier said than done. A tiny dragon like Ito had no problem traversing the thicket of branches and weeds, but for someone as large as Nathan and Nicole, it was a struggle. Branches lashed at Nicole's scales and skinned her wings, and her talons caught on the sides of thick roots. And from all around, the feeling of being watched grew more intense. When on the trail, the watchful eyes seemed distant and less threatening; but here, off the beaten path, Nicole felt their presence surround them. This was their turf, and they were not happy with these uninvited guests.

"I've watched YouTube videos about this place," Nathan said. "Never thought in a thousand years I'd ever venture here."

Nicole said nothing, her mind paralyzed by fear and trepidation.

"I remember one video," Nathan continued, "this guy found a body hanging in the woods. It got taken down, but my friends downloaded it before it got banned and shared it with everyone at school."

"Do you mind?" Nicole said. "I'm already freaked out enough as it is."

"Sorry," Nathan said. "Just thought it would be less scary if we carried on a conversation."

"I don't mind that," Nicole said. "But given the circumstances, I'd like to at least talk about something less gruesome."

"I got it," Nathan said. "What else would you like to talk about, then?"

Nicole paused as she climbed over a downed tree. "What about Omi?" Nicole said. "Daisuke's friendly ghost maid."

Nathan paused and turned around. "The what?"

"Back at his house," Nicole continued. "There's a ghost of a woman named Omi. She makes the beds and does the cooking, and she's a damn good chef if you ask me."

"Hmmm," Nathan said. "If only the ghosts here were so kind." He continued forward, his wings folded tightly against his scales.

Nicole hopped over another log. "At least we know there are good sprits in the world."

"Yeah, and they all seem to avoid this place like the plague." Nathan looked back over his shoulder and then forward again. "Ever feel like you're being watched?" he asked.

"I've been feeling it ever since we started walking," Nicole said. "I'm sure it's just our imagination, though. Right? Right, Nate? It can't be–"

Crunch. Nicole froze. She felt something like bone beneath her talons. Her heart stopped and she gulped. A sickening feeling came over her, and her scales began to crawl.

"Um, Nathan," Nicole said.

"What?"

"I think I stepped on something."

Nathan approached, and in the faint light of the moon, she could see he was confused.

"Okay, and?"

"Could you please take a look for me?" she asked. "I know it sounds weird."

Nathan did as she asked without question, igniting a flame out of his nostril and bending down to inspect where she stood. It didn't take long for the flame to pitter out though. Nathan froze, staring at the spot with a blank expression.

"What is it?" she asked. "Nathan, *tell me.*"

"Don't panic," Nathan said. "Just get off of it."

Nicole lifted her foot and backed away, and before Nathan could stop her, she ignited a spark in her nose to show her what she had stepped on. On the ground, covered in moss and leaves, was a tangled mass of clothes, splayed out like they had been left to the mercy of the elements. In the center of the clothes were yellowed pieces of what looked like bone fragments, and in the center, a human skull.

"Oh god," Nicole cried. She leapt away and grabbed Nathan, burying her head in his shoulder. She could feel the pain and desperation this poor soul must have felt when they were alive, the suffering that led them to such a fate. The forest seemed to weep in tandem, and the air suddenly filled with moaning and wails. Nathan's grasp on her tightened, and when Nicole looked up, she screamed.

All around them, emerging from the trees, were figures dressed in white. They had long bony arms and fingers, long dark hair, and pale, sunken faces. They were whispering to one another in a language that did not sound like Japanese, or any language Nicole had heard. The entities seemed to hover over the ground upon a cloud of milky-white mist that blanketed the forest floor.

And they were closing in on them.

"The yurei," Ito said. Nicole felt him press against her side and could hear the fear in his voice.

"What do we do now?" Nathan asked.

"Run," Ito said.

What started as a sprint turned into a clumsy flight as Nicole surged through the Sea of Trees. She didn't bother looking over her shoulder to see if the yurei were keeping up, for she could feel them approaching, their labored breathing and demonic cries seemingly at her ankles. Nathan attempted to burn them with his flames, but as she expected, the fire did nothing to dampen their pursuit. The flames passed through them harmlessly and only seemed to embolden them with renewed vigor and fury. Their cries grew louder, until they became the only thing Nicole could hear. The forest closed in around her, the trees twisting to grab her and swallow her up. Her vision blurred as ghastly shapes and visions clouded her field of view, and her breath caught in her throat. She dared turn around one last time.

Behind her, the yurei carried themselves on the thick

cloud, their spider-like fingers outstretched, their mouths agape, their eyes milky. They reached for her and Nathan, howled like animals in agony, all while screaming bloody murder. Their long black hair tangled like loose threads and dangled wildly in all directions, while their tattered and torn shrouds floated on the wind. It was the most horrifying sight Nicole had ever seen, a nightmarish scene that instantly scared her forever. She turned back...

A race of pain shot through her body as the trunk of a tree made contact with Nicole's face. Blood pooled into her mouth and nose, seeping into her eyes and stinging them as she fell down, down, down. She heard Ito and Nathan call to her, but it seemed faint. She realized she was falling through a deep pit, the surface retreating from her sight, the cries from above fading as the world around her receded into blackness.

And then, the rocky ground met her at full force.

CHAPTER 19

Nicole pulled herself to her feet, dazed and delirious. She looked up, expecting to see the gaping maw of the cave above, its edges teeming with yurei, but instead, she saw nothing except for the dark ceiling dripping with moisture. For the third time in three days, she was stuck in a cave, only this one contained rock formations with grooves in them like the ripples of a stream.

"Of course," Nicole said to herself. "Lava rock."

She looked around and saw she was alone. No yokai or yurei, no Ito, no Nathan. It was like she had been dropped from the sky and deposited in this strange place without explanation. She peered down the long corridor stretching deep into the earth and anxiously craned her neck to see what was down there. Beyond her line of sight, only darkness prevailed.

"Why do you run?" said a voice in the darkness.

Nicole looked up, expecting to see Typhoon hanging over her, but she was alone. Thinking back, she realized that the voice sounded identical to the one she had heard the day prior, before the Orochi was released.

"Why do you fear me?"

"Who are you?" she asked.

"The one you seek to destroy," said the voice again. "The weapon you seek is nearby, but before you take it, I, Hachi, wish to challenge you."

"To a fight?" Nicole asked, wiping some of the blood from her face.

"No," Hachi said. "I wish to challenge your mind. I see it clouded with violent thoughts, regret, delusions. I feel your hurt, the sadness you feel for your mother, the pain Typhoon forced you to endure. It's turned you hard and bitter, like a ripened fruit before its plucked. But I wish to show you a new path forward, a bridge over the pond of sorrows that have plagued you for so long. I wish to reward you for liberating me, by placing you on a pedestal above all others of your kind, to claim the reward you so desperately deserve."

The cave faded into a cloud of pink and white, and when her vision adjusted, Nicole was standing on a grassy, ethereal plane. Cherry blossom fell around her like snow, while lotuses and orchids grew between Nicole's toes. Ahead of her, a stone bridge arched over a pond that was filled with colorful fish. Nicole stepped onto the bridge and looked down. She saw her reflection mingle with the fish, as petals landed upon the glassy surface.

"This is your home," Hachi said. "All of this is yours. No more Typhoon, no more pain, just eternal serenity. I want to give you this, not just as a token of my admiration, but my heart."

Nicole noticed movement behind her and turned to see the Orochi standing just off to her left. His scales shimmered in the white light, like the tips of frosted leaves, and the expression on each of their eight faces was that of contentment.

"So many dragons have claimed to love you," Hachi said. "Lucca, Tauri, Nathan. But no one can give you what I want to give. I want to thank you for freeing me, and as such, I can give you whatever you want, to treat you as my queen."

The clouds above parted, revealing a statue of Nicole in jade, her wings outstretched to their fullest, the base surrounded with candles and smoldering incense sticks. Below the effigy, dozens of small dragons, with green and white scales, bowed in worship, humming a chant that reverberated reverence.

"You will be worshiped as a god," Hachi said, "immortalized forever among the Kami of this world. Shrines will be erected in your glory, and your name will live on forever on the tongues of our children as one of the greatest dragons who ever lived. And they will inherit the earth and bring forth a new age of dragons, one greater than any bred before."

An image of her and the Orochi lying together in a meadow of soft white grass eclipsed Nicole's vision. She watched as the heads of the beast held her close, while Hachi looked down and doted on her. All around them, their children ran and played, tumbling over each other and flapping their tiny wings. Nicole was taken aback by the beauty she beheld, felt herself drawn to the sight of the Orochi's heads caressing her scales. Nicole, unaware that such a life was possible, let her curiosity roam as she considered this pampered existence as queen to a divine creature. Perhaps it was worth it to leave everything, to leave a cold, hard world, and embrace a life that offered all her heart desired. As she watched the little dragonettes frolic before her, her heart melted, and she felt a yearning, a longing to be with Hachi.

She felt his presence next to her, his breath on her neck. "I love you, Nicole," he whispered. "You delivered me from darkness, and now I wish to do the same for you."

Nicole felt like she was melting. Not even Nathan could give her this much attention. She could almost see herself in this new world the Orochi crafted, a world of pleasure and love. She could almost hear her mother begging her to take it, to say yes to everything the Orochi offered. It made sense, and she felt stupid to question it. For the first time, something in Nicole's life was assured, not left up to chance and circumstances as so much of it had been.

She was about to say yes.

But there was something missing . . .

"What of everyone else?" she asked. "What of my mother, Seth, and Joel? What of Nathan?"

"What of them?"

"What will happen to them?"

"Why does it matter?" Hachi asked, leaning closer. She felt his siblings' necks envelop her. "Do not care for the livelihood of lower beings. Is it wise for wolves to care for pigs and chickens? Are cats responsible for the wellbeing of mice? And does a spider consider the feelings of a fly that gets stuck in its web? They live to provide sustenance, a reason to call ourselves superior. They have no want except to be eliminated by gods like ourselves, to lay down their lives and accept their fate as lesser beings."

Something like blinders fell from Nicole's eyes and the illusion began to sour. She could see clearly the Orochi's plan for all that it was: a lustful pursuit of her scales, a pawn to further another man's goals. It was not an alien feeling; all her life, she had been surrounded by men who wished to control her, exploit her, use her. Her father, Lucca, Tauri, and now Hachi. They were all the same, men who saw little value in her other than what they could get. To them, she was little more than a prop, a token in a game, a toy. Everything was conditional, nothing was for sure, and the cutthroat world Nicole had just managed to escape was back and worse than she remembered.

She felt rage fill her throat, anger pulsate through her veins, fire boil in her chest. She felt stupid for having fallen so easily for this trap, for having been led so far astray, and now she wished to turn back before it was too late.

"You're just like my father," she said, grabbing one of the Orochi's necks, "and I hated him more than anything."

The head hardly had time to react before Nicole bit into it.

* * *

She was back in the cave, like before, but this time she was not alone. This time, there were hundreds, perhaps thousands of piercing white eyes staring at her from floor to ceiling. Their growls and cries of pain signaled to her that the yurei had found and cornered her. She spun around, exhaling a flame in a feeble bid to ward them off, but they moved not an inch. Instead, the fire revealed how truly grotesque the yurei were in person. Their skin was as white as their robes, their mouths wide and dark, their eyes sunken. They seemed to have no thought or feeling behind their eyes, only a hidden desire to spread their misery to anyone in arm's reach. As the last of Nicole's flames extinguished, she caught a glimpse of the passage at the end of the cave and remembered what Hachi had said.

The sword was down there, and it was her only path to salvation.

Nicole sprang to her feet and flew deeper into the cave. She flapped her wings as hard as she could while maintaining a single flame to show her the way. But as she did, the yurei reacted. The cave filled with their screams, an earsplitting symphony of horror that seemed to emit from every crevice. She felt them on her tail, their cold breath lashing her scales as they drew closer. Suddenly, an icy pain raced up her spine, followed by another in her leg, and another on her left wing. She turned and saw three yurei clinging to her, digging their nails into her scales and biting her with their jagged teeth. She tried to shake them off, but all this did was slow her down, and the yurei began to pile onto her. More icy shocks of pain raced through her, and her body stiffened and contorted. Try as she might, she could not possibly fly any further, and she landed hard into a shallow stream.

With their prey down, the yurei went in for the kill. More and more of them piled onto her, until their weight pressed Nicole's head into the water and made it hard for her to breathe. Bloody water filled her mouth as the yurei ripped out her scales and dug their claws into her exposed flesh. She let out a cry, but it was no use. She knew she was dying, and there was no one who could save her.

And she knew that Nathan was next.

Just as Nicole was about to let herself be drowned in a puddle of her own blood, the cave filled with a brilliant white light. The weight of the yurei lifted, and their screams turned to that of terror. Nicole lifted her head and beheld the sight of a woman with wavy, black hair, dressed in a white and red kimono. She was holding a sword above her head, the blade of which glowed a brilliant white. The yurei recoiled in fear as the woman approached, and as she lowered her sword, the creatures released a collective scream of agony. Nicole spun her head around to see the yurei disintegrating, their bodies vanishing into a mist that evaporated with the echoes of their collective voice. With the yurei gone, Nicole's injuries subsided, and she could feel them beginning to heal. The cuts closed up, the blood vanished, her scales grew back, and her strength returned in full.

She turned to the woman, still holding the shimmering blade in the darkness.

"My name is Kushinadahime," the woman said. "Thousands of years ago, the warrior Susanoo pulled this sword out of the original Orochi and gave it to me as a gift. I now present this, the Kusanagi, to you, so you may trap its soul within its blade and end its reign of terror once and for all."

Kushinadahime knelt and presented the Kusanagi to Nicole. Nicole looked the sword over, from the tip of its blade to the bottom of its hilt. Every inch of the sword was made of a hard, white material, like that of bleached bone, which seemed to shimmer and glow in the darkness of the cave. The blade itself was thick and double-edged, while its hilt resembled a spine, the vertebrae fused together and fashioned into a sturdy grip. Gingerly, Nicole touched the smooth side of the blade, its porous surface emitting a subtle warmth that seemed to come from within. The blade did not feel like metal, but like enamel or, more accurately, polished bone.

"Why me?" she asked. "Why would I be picked to wield this awesome weapon?"

"Because you passed the test," Kushinadahime said. "You resisted the Orochi's advances, proved yourself true to your word, and did not turn back on your friends. That is why you were brought to Japan. That is what the clairvoyants in

Hiroshima saw. You are of a chosen few who could withstand the Orochi's promises, and you are one of the only ones who can wield this sword."

Nicole did not know if she understood this completely, nor did she feel like she had the whole story, but all she knew was this was not the time for dithering self-doubt. She grasped the hilt of the Kusanagi and held it up to her eyes. She felt an energy swell though its hilt and into her body. It was as though the sword had fused itself with her somehow, and now it was hers to use however she pleased.

"Good luck," Kushinadahime said. "Pierce the Orochi's heart and imprison it in this blade for all eternity."

Kushinadahime turned and vanished into a cloud of mist, leaving Nicole with the Kusanagi firmly in talon.

CHAPTER 20

Nicole admired the blade a little longer. The Kusanagi felt heavy in her hands, but not too heavy for her to wield effectively. She practiced swinging, jabbing and slashing, the blade making a swooshing noise as she executed a variety of maneuvers. When she felt confident she could take on the Orochi, she set the blade aside and looked around the cavern. Light poured in from a hole in the ceiling, indicating that it was daylight. In the very center of the ray of light, sitting against a rock, was a scabbard made of polished redwood, and fitted to a leather belt. Nicole picked the scabbard up and found it fit the Kusanagi perfectly. As she slid the sword inside and fastened it around her waist, she wondered if she would encounter Kushinadahime again before the war with the Orochi was over.

"Nicole?" said a voice at the other end of the cave. It was Nathan.

Nicole cursed herself for forgetting about him and Ito and called back. "Over here," she said.

Nathan and Ito sprinted towards her from the opposite direction.

"Thank the gods we found you," Ito said.

"We've been looking for you for hours," Nathan said, panting. He hugged Nicole and squeezed her.

"How did you find me?" she asked.

"After we outran the yurei," Ito said, "I followed your scent to a hole in the ground, and we spent practically all night following it."

"All night?" Nicole asked. "I've only been down here less than an hour."

The exhausted look on Nathan's face was all Nicole needed to know that she was wrong in that regard.

"Is that the . . .?" Nathan asked, pointing to the sword.

Nicole nodded. She explained to them how the Kusanagi had come into her possession, and the trials she had endured to retrieve it. As she spoke, Ito examined the sword from top to bottom, looking over every square inch of the weapon to see if it was indeed the weapon they were looking for.

"This is it," Ito said finally. "No doubt about it. It's made of the Orochi's bone, hence its look and feel. And it's consistently warm to the touch. I wouldn't forget the look of the Kusanagi even if I were to grow old and lame."

"Now what do we do?" Nathan asked.

"Simple," Nicole replied, putting the sword back in its scabbard. "We find the Orochi and kill it."

"It can't be that easy, though," Nathan said. "If there's one thing I learned about this life as a dragon, it's that there's always a catch."

Just then, the ground started to shake, and a cloud of dust fell from the ceiling of the cave onto the trio below.

"Oh, come on!" Nathan said. "Was it something I said?"

"Quick," Ito said. "We must evacuate in case of a collapse."

Nicole followed Ito and Nathan as they darted toward the way they came. When they finally reached the surface, Nicole pulled the Kusanagi from its scabbard, ready to slice the Orochi to ribbons. She whirled around, looking for any sign of the creature, but it was nowhere in sight. As the realization came to her, Nicole realized that the shaking had stopped.

"Maybe it was just a small quake," Nicole said.

Before anyone could retort, the roar of jet engines shook everyone to attention. Nicole looked up just in time to see a large military bomber flying overhead, flanked on both sides by a pair of fighter jets.

"Stealth bombers," Nathan said. "They must be on patrol."

"Unless they're heading somewhere," Nicole said. "Ito, can you tell where the Orochi is now?"

"He's just north of here," Ito said, "heading towards Tokyo."

"The same direction the planes are headed," Nicole said. Her talons tightened around the Kusanagi's hilt. "We must follow them before he can attack the capital."

Nathan and Ito both gave her a curious look.

"Nicole," Ito said, "I appreciate your enthusiasm and I'm taken aback by your newfound leadership qualities, but don't you think this is dangerous? Shouldn't we call for support from the rest of the Tokyo Sanctum?"

"I agree," Nicole said. "But we can't let a golden opportunity like this go to waste."

"I'm with Nicole," Nathan said. "This may be the best shot we have at averting a cataclysm. One of us should at least inform the others of our plan, though, so everyone knows what's up. The more support we have, the faster we can counter anything the Orochi attempts."

"That I can do," Ito said. "I'll send a message to every weredragon in Japan, ask them for their support, and tell them to converge on the Orochi's position. I'll also get in touch with the Japanese Self-Defense Forces so that they can coordinate with us and strategize a plan of attack."

Nicole nodded and turned to Nathan. "Need any more time to relax your wings before you take off again?"

As though he were a bird trying to attract a mate, Nathan extended his wings to their broadest point and puffed out his chest. "Never, I'm ready to go when you are, my dear."

Nicole stifled a laugh. She found Nathan's attempts at impressing her with his masculinity somewhat amusing. Little did he know that just by saying yes, he was more of a man than the Orochi could ever hope to be.

"In that case, let's go," Nicole said. "We'll follow the exhaust trails." She turned to Ito. "And if you see my mother anytime soon, tell her that I love her."

Ito nodded, then flapped his tiny wings and took off in the opposite direction. Nicole opened her wings and flapped, and she and Nathan lifted departed the forest.

*   *   *

They flew for most of the day and into the evening. As the hours ticked by, more planes and drones headed past them, and it occurred to Nicole that a plan of some kind was underway. By dusk, a few lights had begun to show down below them, indicating that power had been restored to some, but this was of little comfort. The vast majority of the mainland, as far as Nicole could observe, had been sent back centuries.

By nightfall, the hours of flying caught up with Nicole. Nathan, who by now was ahead, took note of her slowed pace and craned his head back towards her.

"You okay?" he asked. Even though he had spent most of the previous night scampering around looking for her, he seemed like he could go on for a few more hours, much to Nicole's amazement.

"I'm okay," Nicole said. "Just sleepy, that's all."

"Why don't we find a place to crash?" Nathan said. "I think we can both use it."

"No, I can keep going," Nicole lied, blinking back the burning in her eyes and the fatigue in her wings.

"Come on, babe," Nathan said. "You know you can't go on forever. We've both been up for nearly two days now."

He was right, but at the same time, Nicole wanted to go forward. She had to keep going, or else the Orochi would. . .

"Okay," she gasped. "I'll bite. Let's find somewhere to sleep."

They scanned the ground until they found a quiet patch of woods outside a small suburb. They landed atop a soft patch of grass and brushed away some sticks and with their tails to make the area more comfortable. Still in her dragon form, Nicole sprawled out on her back, Nathan next to her, and looked up at the starry sky above. Comets crisscrossed the night, while the forest was filled with the creaking of toads and the grumble of various night creatures.

"Nathan?" Nicole asked.

"Yes?"

"Where do you see us in five years?"

Nathan rolled onto his side and looked at her.

"I hadn't thought of that yet," he said. "To be honest, you're the first person I've had a serious relationship with."

"But where do you think we'll be in five years?" Nicole insisted. "Do you think we can last?"

"I don't see why not," Nathan said. "I can't see anything coming between us anytime soon."

"At least not from either of us," Nicole said. "I can only imagine the sort of outside forces that'll try to tear us apart."

Nathan moved closer to her and put an arm on her shoulder. "I won't let that happen if I can help it."

Nicole put her hand on Nathan's wrist and smiled. "I know you won't," she said. At the same time, though, she couldn't help wondering if powers beyond their control would drive a wedge between them eventually. As long as the Orochi was alive, and smitten with her, their relationship was at risk.

Nathan moved closer but stopped when the scabbard of the Kusanagi poked him.

"Oops," Nathan said, backing away. "My bad."

"Take it off me," Nicole said.

"You sure?" Nathan said. "I figured you'd want it near you."

"I can reach for it if needed," she said. "But I can't sleep with it around my waist."

Nathan got up and started unhooking the belt loops, pulling the leather strap free, and setting the sword and scabbard beside her. Nicole's muscles loosened, and her wings unfurled. She reached up and placed a hand on Nathan's cheek.

"I feel like I can be very vulnerable around you," she said. "Like I can let down my defenses."

"So do I," Nathan said. He leaned over and planted his lips on her forehead, which Nicole returned by wrapping her arms and wings around him.

"I don't want anyone but you," Nicole said, her tail coiling around his.

"Me neither," he said. "Just don't get killed anytime soon."

"I won't as long as you stay alive," she said.

"I will," he said, his lips on hers. "I promise."

"Now, where do you see us in five years?" Nicole asked, as Nathan wrapped her within his wings.

"Here," he said. "In your arms."

CHAPTER 21

Hachi grit his teeth as he flew, the rage boiling inside him like the core of the sun. He always felt anger, yet this felt unique. This was personal. This anger came not from his or any of his brother's brains, but from his heart.

When are we going to stop?

"When I say we can!" Hachi snapped. They were somewhere north of Fukushima, west of Sendi, near Mt. Funagata. The peaks of green mountains poked up from the carpet of clouds, while the first rays of sunlight showed towards the east.

You still long for her. Why? Why pain yourself over a mortal being?

"Because she said 'no'," Hachi said. "I reached out to *her*, chose *her* above all others. She was *my* maiden, the desire of *my* heart, and if I can't have her, no one can!"

You wish to cry. We can feel it.

"I liked you better when your talk was short and simple. Since when can you articulate entire sentences?"

Our intelligence has improved since we hatched, for we have learned along with you.

"Well, why don't you learn to shut the hell up?!"

The other heads retreated from Hachi's mind, allowing him to stew in his anger. Why had she bothered to free him if she didn't want him? Why was she playing this game with his emotions? Didn't she know she was playing with fire, a fire that could consume the entire world?

What are you going to do?

"Kill her. Kill her and Nathan. I'll make her watch as I rip the scales out of her man, one by one, until he's nothing but a pink blob of flesh. Then, once he's bled to death, I'll make her eat his corpse."

Extreme, don't you think?

"Don't question my motives!" Hachi forced them to a stop and hovered, and his brothers turned at to him with looks of confusion. He glared at each of them, his teeth bared, his eyes glowing with the light of white-hot hate.

"I don't care who made her do it. I don't care if Typhoon forced her hand or if she was under any duress. By breaking the egg open, she entered a covenant to be with me forever, and by forsaking it, she must suffer."

This is the first we've heard of this decree. Did you just envision this?

"Silence! I can do as I wish. I am Hachi, the smartest of you all and your leader. If I wish to enforce a rule to address a drastic issue, you must follow it, no matter how abrupt it may seem. Understand?"

As his brothers pondered this sudden change in motivation, Hachi saw movement from the corner of his eye. He looked and saw the rays of the sun bend like it would around a glass object. Hachi focused on the spot, and there it was again. Against the blue-black horizon, a transparent shape circled them.

"What is that?" he said.

Suddenly, the shape materialized into a black figure resembling a large bird. It was pointed at the nose, with a pair of wings stretching out and backwards. Bright rockets glowed as the craft accelerated and tilted, revealing 'RG-X84' printed in white along the side.

Another bomb craft. We must run.

"No," Hachi said. "We must fight. If we don't stand our ground, the humans, and Nicole, will never learn to fear us."

The X84 turned and hovered in front of them, a pair of large cannons pointed directly at their chest. As they stared, the cannons started to rotate, creating a buzzing noise that reminded Hachi of a swarm of bees.

"Dive!" Hachi yelled, just as a barrage of cannon fire whizzed over them. They dove towards the mountains, the strange craft hot on their tail, its guns firing at a thousand rounds a minute. They bobbed and weaved as white-hot bolts split the air around their heads. Hachi felt their wings beat faster and faster, their joints growing sore, but the X84 never gave up for a second.

"Such magic!" Hachi said. "Human ingenuity will never cease to amaze me."

Before the other heads could respond, there came from behind a whoosh, and a bang. The wind was knocked out of Hachi and he and his brothers tumbled through the sky to the ground below. They landed with a crash on the side of a mountain, sending chunks of rock, dirt, and trees into the air. When the dust settled, Hachi looked up and coughed up a mouthful of blood.

We're injured. We must retreat.

Hachi scanned the skies, but the X84 was nowhere in sight.

"It's vanished again," he said.

Ichi, the first head, rolled his eyes into the back of his head and sniffed the air above him, and Hachi coaxed his brothers to duck and melt into the trees. While his siblings attempted to make themselves small, Hachi studied Ichi's face, which had hardened in a look of intense concentration.

It's coming closer. Smells like ozone.

"We haven't flown that high in almost a millennium. How do you remember that scent?"

The thoughts of the other heads fell silent, and Hachi joined Ichi in scanning the sky.

Suddenly, Ichi's neck stiffened and he pointed his nose towards a spot above them.

"There!" Hachi cried. "Charge!"

They leapt and followed Ichi's gaze. Hachi felt their body slam against the X84's metal shell, and their necks wrapped around it like a boa constrictor. Hachi and his brothers dug their fangs into the shell and peeled it back to expose its innards.

No humans.

"It's controlled with pure magic," Hachi said. "A human mage must be powering it from thousands of miles away because they're too cowardly to face us in person."

Suddenly, a large metal cylinder shot out from the top of the craft. Propelled by rockets, the cylinder collided with Hachi's face on its voyage up. The X84 gradually lost power, until its rockets began to sputter and die. Hachi shook himself and looked up at the silver cylinder, its exterior coated in yellow and orange symbols.

"The magic is held in there!" Hachi said. "Quick! I want it!"

They let go of the X84, leaving it to plummet lifelessly to earth, and charged after the cylinder. The Orochi flapped their wings as quickly as they could, watching the rockets start to dim as it reached the part where sky turned to space. Finally, the Orochi grabbed it with their talons, clutching it tightly as the rockets died. Using their wings to hover, Hachi examined the symbols printed on the sides of the cylinder, and tried to use his cursory knowledge of human languages to decipher what any of the words meant.

What does the trefoil mean?

"Must be how humans classify this type of magic." He squinted at the writing. "Ray-de-oh-act-tive. Hmmm. I've never heard of this magic before. Must be a new type that was conjured after we were–"

Hachi was engulfed by a blinding white light. Heat burned his scales down to his flesh and incinerated his wings. The heads of his brothers were vaporized, leaving him maimed and disfigured. He felt his charred body drop, felt the impact as he slammed into the ground. His vision gone, Hachi plummeted down a round, dark tunnel. He had gone down this last when the warrior Susanoo ended his life after playing him dirty. He knew what was next; the egg, and his life would start again, whenever that would be. Hachi did not resist death's pull. He knew it was pointless to fight his cycle of death and rebirth, no matter how he longed to break it.

But then, something pulled him back. He felt his scales grow and harden, his wings reform, his body grow strong. He felt his brothers' necks grow back and surpass their original size. Hachi felt their body stretch and grow outward, while a heat brewed inside them, like fire in their belly. Hachi opened his eyes, saw the crater they made, saw his brothers, asleep, but alive, and then he saw the state of their body.

"My brothers, wake up!" Hachi said. "We've grown. We're

almost twice as large as we were before."

The other heads opened their eyes and looked upon their body with amazement.

We're unstoppable now.

Hachi flapped their wings and lifted into the air, and the wind they generated blew the trees sideways and sent clouds of dust rolling over the hills.

The yokai watch us with intent.

"That's because we are the alpha predator of the entire world. The most formidable of the yokai, stronger than any spirits, of any beings living or dead. They watch us now out of fear, trepidation, and wonder."

Hachi felt them staring at them from below, their teeming, little eyes watching from every crevice and every shadow. They watched, and waited for his command.

"The oni, the ikuchi, the gashadokuro will respect us now, and follow our orders in defiance of Ito and his ilk. Together, we shall form an army unlike any the world has ever seen, and the powers that be will have no option but to bow before us!"

Hachi and his brothers exhaled jets of white-hot fire into the clouds as the yokai below them cried and shrieked. When they were done, the light faded, dark clouds rolled in, and the sound of thunder rumbled over the mountains.

"Onward, my brothers, to Tokyo."

CHAPTER 22

Nicole and Nathan didn't get much sleep that night. After they were finished having their fun Nicole told Nathan of Hachi's plans, and how he tried to tempt her. As Nicole spoke of how she rejected his advances, she noticed a change in Nathan. It was like his heart had melted in his chest and his scales turned to honey. He smiled meekly and slid closer to Nicole.

"You really said all that?" he asked. "Even after he offered to make you a goddess?"

Nicole nodded. "All my life, men have been trying to use me to advance their own goals and agendas. My father, my brother, and most of my friends when I was growing up. But you're not like that. I know you love me for who I am, not what I can give you."

"That's the same way I feel about you," Nathan said. "You chose me when so many others looked the other way, and for that, I cannot thank you enough."

Nicole smiled and kissed Nathan on the forehead. "Where do you see yourself when this is all over?"

Nathan laughed and put his wings around her. "Oh, I see where this is going."

"No, I mean it this time," Nicole said. "Where do you see yourself after the Orochi is dead and gone?"

Nathan paused midway. "I haven't given it much thought.

College, I guess. Maybe get an apartment of our own."

"I want to get my GED," Nicole said. "Then sometime down the road . . ."

Nicole trailed off when she saw the expression on Nathan's face. Before she could ask what was wrong, a pair of thick arms wrapped around her throat and ripped her from Nathan's arms. She was dragged backwards across the ground, her talons digging into the soil and whatever she could grab. Her feet brushed against the Kusanagi and she grabbed the scabbard with her toes. Hoisting it up, she grasped the scabbard and used the butt of the sword to bash her attacker in the head. Her attacker let go, and Nicole sprang to her feet, drawing the Kusanagi. But as she prepared herself to slice her attacker, she noticed that it was an oni, like the one she encountered in Ito's cave. The oni cradled his nose with both hands, and for a moment Nicole thought she had made a mistake. But as the creature recovered, it eyed her with a look of pure malice.

Before it could attack again, Nicole ran it through, coating the Kusanagi's blade with a sheet of green blood. From behind her, she heard Nathan scream, and she turned to see three oni attacking him. One of them had him in a headlock, while the others approached, brandishing clubs and crude blades. Nicole dashed over, but before she could intervene, a flame burst from Nathan's mouth and engulfed the oni. Nathan wiggled out of his attacker's arms, threw the creature over his shoulder, and delivered a fatal stomp to its face.

Nathan brushed himself off and glanced at Nicole. "What the hell happened? I thought they were on our side."

Nicole opened her mouth to respond, but she was cut off by a sudden, far-off noise.

Gachi gachi. Gachi gachi.

It sounded like a rattle, like old sticks and stones being thrown around in a burlap sack. The ground shook in rhythmic thumps, like footsteps, and the nesting birds above fluttered away in waves. A shape appeared on the horizon, a slick sphere against the backdrop of the sunrise. As it came into focus, Nicole realized this figure was a giant human skull, atop an equally large skeleton. The thing towered over her and Nathan, and seemed to stare at them with its large, hollow eyes that glowed like balls of fire.

The skeleton stopped and peered down at them, its teeth rattling as it moved. *Gachi gachi. Gachi gachi.* Nicole raised her sword, thinking of a way to attack, but before she could decide, the skeleton was engulfed by flame. Several serpentine dragons flew overhead, dousing it in yellow fire, while the being let out a horrid cry of pain. Nicole watched as the dragons surrounded the creature, just out of reach of its long, slender arms it waved helplessly around in a state of confusion. Realizing these dragons were their allies, Nicole lifted into the air and exhaled a jet of fire onto the beast, adding to its misery. Nathan joined her, and together they roasted the skeleton alive and turned its bones ashy and black.

Just when it seemed the creature was done for, it managed to grab the tail of one of the dragons overhead. The dragon struggled to break free, kicking and clawing at the bony hand, while the creature raised it to its opened maw. Nicole choked on her fire when she realized the dragon was Daisuke. Without thinking, she dived towards the creature and shattered the skull with a mighty swing of the Kusanagi. A shower of bone and teeth rained down on Nicole as the creature released Daisuke and collapsed into a flaming heap.

The dragons regrouped in a clearing next to the scene of the carnage. Among them was Daisuke, Seth, and Ito, along with her mother, who stood apart from the rest of the group like she was eager to leave.

"What the hell is going on?" Nicole asked.

"Quite a bit, to put it lightly," Seth said.

"Let me explain," Ito said, stepping forward. "A few hours ago, the Orochi took down an unmanned, experimental aircraft that was powered by a radioactive turbine. After destroying it, the creature absorbed the radiation in its core and this caused the Orochi to grow in both size and power. Now it has intimidated the yokai into following its every command and sent them on a rampage across the continent."

"But that's not the worst of it," Daisuke said. "The US Military held a press conference this morning, and announced it is planning to use nuclear weapons against the Orochi as a last-ditch effort to destroy it. The monster is headed towards Tokyo, and the military plans to level the city if it chooses to stay there."

"And to make matters even worse," Seth added, "the Japanese and US governments are giving all of Japan 72 hours to evacuate to avoid fallout, and they can only evacuate by air, because a bunch of giant serpents called the *ikuchi* decided to join our eight-headed friend and attack every ship in the Atlantic. There's no possible way they can get everyone out in time, and both governments are planning for a mass casualty event, the likes of which haven't been seen since the end of the Second World War."

"But at least you have the Kusanagi," Daisuke said. Nicole handed it to him so he could observe it. "This sword, and your wits, are the key to this nation's survival, and the survival of the whole world."

Nicole was about to respond but was cut off by her mother.

"Good, you've got your damn sword, now leave my daughter alone."

Chyanne grabbed Nicole by the wrist and jerked her away.

"Mom, what are you doing?"

"We're leaving," Chyanne said. "We're going anywhere but here, and you're not looking back."

"But-"

"But nothing!" Chyanne glared at Seth and Nathan. "I trusted you, Seth, to keep my daughter safe, and instead you've gotten her involved in not one, but two calamities that could have cost her her life. And you. . ." Chyanne pointed an incriminating talon at Nathan. "Stay the hell away from my daughter. You've been nothing but a nuisance to her the moment she met you."

Nicole pulled herself away and held firm. "No," she said. "I love him, and these are my friends, and I'm going to stay here and help them."

Chyanne stood with a vexed expression, her lips set in firm disapproval, her eyes glowing with bitterness.

"Are you trying to destroy me?" Chyanne growled. "I spent my whole life trying to protect you, and ever since you met that boy, your life has been a constant battle for survival. But not anymore. The army has a plan, and you found the sword. We can leave now and get you out of this shit show once and for all."

Chyanne started to leave, but Nicole held her ground.

"If you want to walk out of my life again, go ahead," Nicole said. "If the last decade has taught me anything, it's that I can take care of myself without you."

Chyanne stopped and turned her head around, slowly.

Nicole continued, "If this is your way of trying to make up for the last ten years, then you're too late. I'm not the scared little girl I was when you handed me over to Seth and Joel. I'm not some defenseless princess in need of a protector. I'm a grown woman who can make my own decisions for myself, and if I want to stay behind and prevent a cataclysm, I'll do it."

"Hey babe," Nathan interjected, "you think you want to tone it down a–"

"And if I want to be with this man," Nicole said, wrapping her arms around Nathan, "and if I want to quicken with him, then that's my decision. No one controls me anymore, not the Orochi, not my father, and especially not you!"

Nicole expected her mother to deliver a stinging retort, but instead, Chyanne fell silent. She looked at Nicole with a pained expression, her jaw agape, her eyes moist. She let out a labored breath, sniffled, and swallowed back her tears.

"Everything I've done," Chyanne said, "since the day you were born, was to protect you. I've done my job, my time as a mother has come to an end, and now I see I am no longer needed." She turned east and spread her wings. "Goodbye, my dear daughter. I'll always love you."

Chyanne took off, and Nicole, released from her anger, flew

after her. but her mother's wingbeats were too fast, and before long, she was just a speck on the horizon.

"Where is she going?" Nathan asked when she landed.

"Back to Hong Kong," Nicole said. "What have I done, Nathan? I've just lost my mother after so long and . . ."

Nathan held out his hand. "Let's go talk somewhere private," he said.

She took it, and they ventured into the woods.

* * *

When they were far enough away from prying ears, Nathan spoke.

"I sensed that came from a place of pain," he said.

Nicole nodded. "It's been hard for me to process all of this," she said. "Years ago, back when Seth told me my mother had taken her life, I was stricken with grief, but I was also angry. I felt abandoned, lost, and when I found out my mother was alive, a part of me was furious that she hadn't contacted me when she had the chance."

"I know the feeling," Nathan said. "The feeling of being cheated, as though you were denied a shot at a normal life."

"Did you feel that way when your dad died?"

Nathan nodded. "I was young, so I didn't understand what was happening. And for the first few years I was angry, because I thought maybe if my dad had taken better care of himself, he wouldn't have died so young. And then, just before my forever flu hit, I resented the fact that my mother never remarried, because I missed having a dad.

"But then I adapted. I learned that circumstances had given me a bad hand, and all I could do was try and overcome it the best I could. So I reconciled my anger and used it to help build my strength and be the best I could be."

Nathan stopped and looked Nicole in the eye. "Both of us were dealt a bad hand in life. Both of us come from dysfunctional families that often left us feeling cold and unloved, and it's okay to be angry. That anger made us stronger, and it is with that strength that we are able to overcome our weaknesses and grow as people and dragons. You're the strongest woman I've ever met, and I know you can achieve wonderful things, with or without your mom by your side. That doesn't mean you can't love her, but you can move on from the loss."

Nicole bowed her head and let out a sigh. "You're right," she said. "I'm glad I was able to get that off my chest, but I need to move forward. Like my mother said, she's done her job." She looked up and locked eyes with the love of her life. "Now it's time to do mine."

Nathan smiled. "I do have one request, though."

"What's that?"

"Please don't quicken yet," he said. "I'm not even old enough to drink, let alone be a father."

Nicole laughed. "I wasn't serious about that, but if things keep going the way they are, who knows."

Nathan nudged her with his snout, while Nicole leaned forward until their foreheads were together.

"In time, my dear," Nathan said. "In time."

CHAPTER 23

Typhoon, under his facade of Silvio Contti, sat in his hotel room in Tokyo and watched as the world fell apart. He was on the edge of a large bed, a glass of champagne in hand, listening as his bucket of iced Bollinger rattled as helicopters and military planes roared overhead. He just got out of the jacuzzi tub, and the bathrobe he wore was still damp as he let the air from outside dry him. Through the open sliding-glass door, sirens blared, soldiers screamed into megaphones, police whistles screeched, and pedestrians shouted in confusion. Somewhere outside, a car drove up and down the street in front of the hotel, blaring a message in Japanese, English, Chinese, and Korean.

Attention! Attention! This is a message from the Ministry of Defense. The Prime Minister has ordered the complete evacuation of the Tokyo metropolitan area. All residents are to follow the orders of security personnel and follow posted directions. Please remain calm and do not attempt to defy the evacuation order for your own safety.

"Easier said than done," Typhoon said, taking a sip from his glass.

On the other side of his door, Typhoon heard people running down the hall, their luggage banging against the sides of the corridor as they hurried to the emergency exit. Typhoon took one last look around his expensive room, recalling his time on earth and everything that had led to this moment. He shook his head and kicked off his fuzzy slippers.

Outside, the sky darkened, and the screams of the populace grew in volume. Typhoon gulped the last of his champagne and sauntered over to the balcony. To the north of the city, dark clouds enveloped the horizon, emitting bolts of white lightning that cracked with defining thunder. Large skeletons, *gashadokuro*, rose from between the skyscrapers and began marching south. Below him, civilians ran in the opposite direction, knocking over police barricades in defiance of protocol. From the north, the howls of oni and the hiss of ikuchi filled the air, all the while heavy wingbeats carried over the city like the beating of a heart.

The Orochi appeared towards the rear of the march, its wings gliding over the city and kicking up a storm of dust and debris. The beast flew over the hotel, and the building quaked in its wake, while cars, traffic lights, and bits of rubble slammed against its walls and shattered its windows. The Orochi circled in the air to Typhoon's right, killed its speed, and dropped out of the sky, sending shockwaves through the city as it landed. The Orochi let out a roar that echoed far and wide, and its heads spat torrential fire, engulfing everything it touched.

Typhoon shook his head. He tossed his glass over the railing and undid his bathrobe, letting the blistering air and sparks lick his naked flesh. He climbed over the side, let go, and was in his dragon form before he reached the ground.

Typhoon flew towards the Orochi as oni and gashadokuro looked on. Below him, orange flames rose higher, and columns of smoke joined the black skies above to create an inky smog that blotted out the sun. Typhoon calmly approached the Orochi, unafraid of this show of force. He hardly jumped when a large, serpentine ikuchi sprang from his left and inserted itself between him and the Orochi. Its forked tongue flicked, and the creature emitted a hiss through jaws filled with razor sharp teeth. The creature looked ready to snap, but Typhoon showed no fear. He could burn this pitiful worm with his mind if he wanted.

"At ease," Hachi said.

The ikuchi glared at Typhoon and lowered itself. Typhoon flew up to the Orochi and hovered just outside of striking distance from its eight jaws.

"Care to congratulate me?" Hachi asked. "Or are you here to gloat like you always do?"

"Neither," Typhoon said. "You're fulfilling your purpose in life: to destroy and conquer without mercy or regret. With or without my guiding hand, you're doing exactly what I created you to do."

Hachi laughed. "You still wish to take credit for something I've done of my own accord. Typical Typhoon, always raining on other's parades for the sake of his gluttonous ego."

"I know you inside and out," Typhoon said, "and none of this surprises me. It resembles what I had in store for you, except I would have done it in a more exact way."

"Which is what?"

"Attack the capitals of the five most powerful nations on earth, rather than spend your time attacking a city that poses no threat to you."

"What's this?" Hachi said. "Morals? Typhoon has a moral code now? What's next? Nuclear disarmament?"

"I may be a tyrant," Typhoon said, "but I'm a smart one. Without my dictation, you are just a monster, an aimless drone living by your own cognition, without a goal except to thirst for mortal flesh and to pillage the world with no goal, no endpoint."

"How do you know I have no endpoint?" Hachi snapped. "How do you know I won't succeed where you failed?"

"At what?" Typhoon said. "Getting Nicole to love you? That ship has sailed, son. You have no hope of getting her to love you any more than I have getting Nathan to be my protege."

"Then she'll die!" Hachi spat. "And Nathan will die with her, and everyone who defies me will die and I shall become the most powerful being in the universe!"

"And then what?" Typhoon asked. "When all the bombs have dropped, and all the people are dead, then what will you do?"

Typhoon turned north and flew away.

"I'm not done with you yet!" Hachi called.

"We were done the moment you hatched," Typhoon replied, more to himself than anyone else.

CHAPTER 24

Nicole stood on the rooftop of an apartment block in one of the northern wards of the Tokyo metropolitan area. She was joined by Nathan, Seth, and Daisuke, who sat on their haunches in their dragon forms and watched the scene below. Towards the south, where the city met the harbor, the Orochi stood conversing with his allies as though they were deciding their next steps. The night sky was alight with roaring flames that made the clouds above shimmer with yellow light. Below her, the Japanese Ground Self Defense Forces had amassed a small garrison, with tanks and armored vehicles standing in wait. Above them, dual-blade helicopters roared, and the sound of evacuating aircraft faded into the distance.

And among the planes and helicopters that crisscrossed the sky, an army of serpentine dragons flew this way and that, eventually settling along the rooftops of the northern wards.

Nicole gripped the hilt of the Kusanagi; she was so close to ending this all, and yet here she was, waiting. She clenched her teeth and growled, her scales bristling. As if he noticed, Nathan entwined his tail with hers and squeezed. The sensation made Nicole feel a little better, but the only thing that could ease her tension was thrusting her blade into the Orochi's chest.

Daisuke turned to face them, his expression blank and void of emotion.

"We can't expect to attack it head-on," he said. "That would be suicide. We need something of a diversion to stun the Orochi and allow us to attack."

"That's what we've been trying to tell the army," Nathan complained. "But they won't do anything to help us."

"Like they have anything," Nicole said. "You could throw every army in the world at that eight-headed bastard and he'd still come out on top."

"And we can't sacrifice any more dragons," Daisuke said. "I know the Tokyo Sanctum is united on this front, but throwing our kin at the situation and hoping for a result is not going to change anything."

Nicole heard tiny wingbeats from the opposite end of the balcony and turned to see Ito flying up to meet them.

"Bad news," he said. "The US Air Force is moving their attack up by three days."

"Wait," Nathan said, counting on his fingers. His eyes grew wide when the realization hit him. "That means they're going to strike tomorrow! How do they expect to evacuate such a big city in so little time?"

"They don't," said a voice behind them. Nicole glanced over her shoulder and saw a gruff-looking Japanese man in military fatigues. "The US Department of Defense has accepted the fact that collateral damage is an inevitability." The man paused and bowed to Nicole. "Pardon me, Ms. Newheart. My name is General Jun Fukuda of the Japanese Ground Self Defense Force. I have been placed in charge of evacuating the Tokyo metropolitan area and the surrounding wards. My apologies for the distressing news. I can understand your frustration."

"Frustration is an understatement," Nicole spat. "How could they do this? Don't they know there are lives at stake?"

"They're aware," the General said. "However, China and Russia have been accusing the US of dragging their feet on the Orochi situation and are threatening to take matters into their own hands. Moscow in particular is worried the Orochi will attack Vladivostok and they're threatening a ground invasion of Japan unless the US does something first."

"So, they've bowed to political pressure," Seth said. "What a joke."

"It's just like Hiroshima and Nagasaki," Daisuke said. "The US wants to show the world how strong they are, and we're stuck in the middle."

"Can't we delay them?" Nathan said. "Don't they know our plan? Don't they know this will only make the Orochi stronger?"

General Fukuda shook his head. "The President has already signed off and submitted the launch codes. There's nothing we can do to stop it. The best you can do now is escape while you still have the chance."

Nicole felt her heart sink. She glanced towards the Orochi in the distance, its heads hanging like the branches of a weeping willow. She bit her lip and cursed the monster under her breath, furious that in spite of everything she had done, Hachi was going to escape justice.

"When will it happen?" Nicole asked.

"Tomorrow night," the General said. "Before midnight."

"So, there's still a chance we can do something," Daisuke said.

"It'll have to be quick," Seth said. "But if I'm not mistaken, it looks like our friend over there is starting to get sleepy."

Nicole glanced over her shoulder again and noticed how more of the heads were beginning to sag, and that Hachi was starting to sway.

"If we can wait until it falls asleep," Nicole said, "we can strike with little resistance."

"But what about his goons?" Nathan said. "They don't look tired. They look like they can pull a Lionel Ritchie and keep going all night long."

"I could inquire about the means of ordering an airstrike," General Fukuda said. "But that might wake the Orochi up, and my contemporaries in the Air Self Defense Force might not be keen on putting themselves in harm's way."

"We may not be able to get around waking it up," Nicole

said, "but we can neutralize the yokai under his command, and then it'll be easier for me to focus my energy on the Orochi."

Daisuke stepped forward. "And I can rouse the dragons under my command to assist the Air Self Defense, so they don't need to put as many of their pilots at risk."

"But will they agree to that?" Nicole asked. "You said it yourself you don't want to sacrifice too many of your countrymen."

"Not unless they have friends in high places."

Nicole felt her heart flutter at the sound of the voice. She whipped her head around and saw the green scales and soft, amber eyes that belonged to none other than Joel Urch. He was hovering in the sky above the apartment block, at the head of a whole host of dragons, most of whom were serpentine. But there were many others who appeared to be of western origin, and some of whom she recognized. She saw Nathan's aunts, Tiffany and Tina Cuthbert, his uncles, Simon and Toby, and his grandfather Lionel.

"Grandpa?" Nathan asked, surprised. "What are you all doing here?"

"Well, the 24-hour news cycle exists for a reason," Lionel said, his gold scales basking in the light from below. "And the DC Sanctum felt that our brothers and sisters in Japan could use a hand."

"Joel, you son of a bitch," Seth said through a grin. "How the hell did you all get here?"

"Booked a flight to Seoul," Joel said, "then we took the rest of the trip by wing. We even managed to recruit some members of the Seoul Sanctum to assist in the effort." Joel nodded to the serpentine dragons surrounding them.

An emerald-green dragon who Nicole also recognized flew forward and landed upon the roof.

"Mr. Ikeda," she said, bowing to Daisuke. "My name is Eugenia Mokvoich, leader of the Washington DC Sanctum. I would like to offer you my services in helping you repel this threat to your homeland."

"Ms. Mokvoich," Daisuke said. "I appreciate your assistance. We're formulating a plan to help Nicole fulfill her divine destiny to kill the Orochi."

All eyes turned to Nicole, who smiled meekly in response.

"I was given a sword," she said, "which just so happens to be the only weapon in the world that can kill it."

"A goddess handed it to her," Nathan said. "And it was taken from the neck of the original Orochi thousands of years ago."

Nicole could see everyone's eyes move to the scabbard around her waist, and she knew she couldn't turn down their curiosity. She drew the sword and held it up for everyone to observe.

"Holy mackerel," Joel said. "How did this all come about?"

Nicole told them everything, explaining her connection with the mystical sword, and detailing their plan of attack. When she was done, Nicole put the sword back in its scabbard and waited for a response.

"Sounds like we came at the right time," Joel said. "Maybe we can help provide air support."

"I think that would be helpful," Daisuke said. "Now, all we need is the support of the JSDF and I think we have something feasible."

Nicole turned to General Fukuda, who looked overwhelmed by his audience of dragons.

"I can put a call out," he said, "and while I can't guarantee anything, I can tell you that there are a lot of proud soldiers in the JSDF who are not content with the American response. Let me get on it right away, and I'll let everyone know as soon as possible."

He bowed to those present before disappearing into the opening at the top of the stairs and vanishing into the apartment block. When he was out of sight, Ito stepped forward to address the rest of the dragons.

"If I may be of help," he said, "there are many yokai who still listen to me. I can summon them and have them come to our aid. In particular, I can summon the *ryu* to assist us.”

“Who are they?” Nathan asked.

“Dragons, like you and me, but with magical intuition,” Ito said. “Some say they are the spirits of dragons who passed on, and they can be a source of good luck and fortune.”

“Well, good luck is something we can all use,” Joel said. “I say go for it.”

“I can’t tell you how much we appreciate this,” Nicole said looking to the new arrivals.

“Don’t mention it,” Tina replied. “Your part of our family now, and we’ll do anything for one of our own.”

Nicole smiled and felt a weight lift from her shoulders. She glanced up at the stars and said a quick prayer to Blizzard, thanking her for restoring the hope that she thought had long since abandoned them.

“Well,” Nathan said, “when can we start?”

Nicole looked back at the Orochi; Hachi was the only head showing any sign of life, with the rest asleep.

“Soon,” she said. “Very soon.”

CHAPTER 25

But it wasn't soon enough.

Despite tendrils of fatigue that had lulled him, Hachi refused to sleep. All throughout the night, Nicole watched the Orochi start to doze off, but each time it seemed Hachi had given in to sleep, the eighth head would jerk itself awake. Around midnight, the Orochi forced itself to walk towards the Tokyo Skytree, where Hachi wrapped his head and wings around the tall, steel tower. There, with his brothers' heads dangling below him, Hachi attempted to prop himself up and force himself to stay awake. But even this seemed futile to Nicole, and as the hours ticked on, Hachi's eyes grew heavy, and eventually, he too fell asleep.

As the first rays of sunlight bathed Tokyo in a golden haze, Nicole turned to the dragons who had settled in a large parking garage at the foot of an office complex where the JSDF was posted. She found Nathan sleeping near an overlook on the second level, using an abandoned taxi as a pillow. She nudged him awake, and Nathan yawned and stretched his legs.

"Good morning," he said. "Where were you all night?"

"With the army," Nicole said, "watching Hachi. He finally fell asleep."

Nathan pulled himself to his feet and shook himself. "When do we strike?"

"Soon," Nicole said. "And this time I mean it."

Some of the other dragons were beginning to stir as sunlight pierced through the openings of the car park. From floors below, there came the rumbling of an engine, and from around a corner there emerged an all-terrain vehicle covered in camouflage. The vehicle stopped in front of Nicole and Nathan and General Fukuda stepped out.

"The strike is beginning in forty-five minutes," he said. "I suggest you get your people up and ready in advance."

"Thank you, General," Nicole said. "But what about the Skytree? Aren't you concerned about damaging it?"

The General shook his head solemnly. "Sacrifices have to be made," he said, "and the Defense Forces have made it clear: spare nothing."

Nicole nodded as the General climbed back into his transport and descended to the lower levels.

"Are you ready for this?" Nathan said.

"Ready as I'll ever be," Nicole replied, though she didn't think she was. She was tired from the long days and nights that had preceded her, was stressed over her mother's sudden departure, and was scared of what was next. But like any trial of life, this was unavoidable, and there was no turning back now. Mentally, she prepared herself for what was ahead, hoping beyond hope no one would be killed, though she knew that the risk would be tremendous.

Nathan lifted the taxi and handed Nicole the Kusanagi, which she had left in his care the night prior. Nicole fastened it around her waist just as she noticed Joel, Seth, and Daisuke making their way down the ramp to where she stood.

"Took him long enough to fall asleep," Seth quipped. "I should imagine he'll get a nice, rude awakening."

"Is everyone ready?" Nicole asked.

Daisuke nodded as several of his dragons departed the car park and flew up to the towers above. "I briefed them before we went to sleep. They have everything ready, as does Ito, who has summoned his ryu in preparation."

"And we know what we're going to do," Joel said, gesturing

to the winged dragons who mingled in the skies next to the serpentine ones. "We're going to follow the local's lead, let them take charge, and assist them with whatever they need."

Nicole took a deep breath and tightened the straps of her scabbard. "Then I guess we're ready to fly." She turned her attention to Joel. "The Orochi is resting against the Tokyo Skytree, and the JSDF has authorized its destruction. Once it's down, that's when I'll strike."

"That tower will bury it alive," Daisuke said. "It may even render it immobile."

"We can hope," Seth said. He climbed onto the edge of the parking garage. "Let's go gang."

Seth led the way to their agreed-upon waypoint: the base of a five-story pagoda that sat opposite the Skytree on the other end of the Sumida River. The pagoda was next to a Buddhist temple called Senso-ji, the monks of whom were already awake and praying for a miracle. With the monk's permission, Daisuke and several dragons from the Tokyo and Seol Sanctums joined them. They ascended the temple stairs and recited their rhythmic chant, in sync with the monk's lead. All the while, Nicole kept her eyes fixed on the tower, looming over the horizon, and the sleeping giant that lay in its wake. To her, the Skytree looked like the CN Tower in Toronto, only taller and more imposing.

"This place has changed so much since the last time I was here," Seth said.

"When was that?" Nathan asked.

"Before the Second World War," Seth said. "Tokyo looked a lot different then. It's almost unrecognizable now, and yet, there are still remnants of the past here and there." He glanced over to the temple. "I couldn't think of another place on earth where the traditional and the modern come together in such harmony."

Joel laughed. "What, are the old brownstones in Greenwich not enough for you?"

Seth turned his eyes toward Joel and smiled. "I missed you, ol' pal. Thanks for coming with reinforcements."

"Anytime, old fella," Joel said.

Nicole lifted her head and felt the breeze from the water caress her scales. The city was strangely silent: no traffic, no people, not a peep. It was as though someone had pressed pause and the city ground to a halt. She wondered if this was how it was back in ancient times, when humans first met dragons.

"What are you thinking?" Nathan asked.

"Nothing," Nicole said. "Just waiting."

Nathan put his wing over her. "It's agonizing, isn't it," he said. "It's like waiting for exam scores at the end of the semester."

"Is that what it feels like?" Nicole said. "Guess I'll have to get used to it."

Nathan glanced at her curiously. "So, you are going to get your GED when you get back to the states? It's not going to be easy."

"If I can survive this, then I can survive anything," Nicole said.

Nathan smiled. "And I'll help you however I can."

Out in the distance, the roar of a plane engine wafted over the desolate streets. The praying from the temple stopped and monks and dragons alike gathered by the base of the pagoda to watch. Nicole saw movement in the corner of her eye and saw a large, silver airplane with the Japanese rising sun stamped on the side, flanked by two fighter planes. The yokai on the ground began howling and screaming, desperately trying to wake their leader, but the Orochi remained dead to the world. The armada unleashed their payload, carpet bombing the area leading up to the Skytree. The ground shook as the bombs detonated and the air was filled with sounds of glass shattering and buildings crumbling. The planes reached the Orochi and the bombs detonated at the base of the tower, bathing the beast in fire and causing the Skytree to lean. With their payload exhausted, the trio of planes flew out of sight.

Now, it was the dragons' turn to shine.

From all corners of the city, dragons of every shape, size,

and color descended upon the Orochi. They let out streams of fire onto him and his minions, adding to the fire that was already raging at the base of the Skytree. Nicole could hear the pained cries of the gashadokuro, and the howls of the oni. Suddenly, the river ahead of them swelled and a large, serpentine ikuchi rose to block their view of the carnage. The snake-like creature glared at Nicole and released an evil hiss, but before it could strike, four ryu dragons descended upon it, biting and clawing and forcing it back into the water. The creature cried as waves sprang up in its wake and bloody water flowed through the streets into the temple's courtyard.

All throughout the chaos, Hachi had barely stirred. The head swung lazily from side to side, taking in everything through a pair of heavy eyelids. All the while, the Skytree was beginning to sway more heavily to the right, its steel frame cracking and buckling. There was a loud crash, and the top portion of the Skytree caved in on itself. Hachi's eyes burst open, but before he could utter anything, the tower collapsed, burying the Orochi in a cloud of dust and rubble.

Nicole took out the Kusanagi and pointed it in the air.

"Attack!" she screamed and took flight.

CHAPTER 26

Nicole flew towards the smoldering pile of rubble, sword at the ready, her knuckles tight around its hilt. When the dust cleared, the pile of metal heaved, and the Orochi, with all eight heads screaming in unison, threw it off. Hachi looked positively enraged, his eyes red with pain and fury. The back of his throat began to glow, and he and his brothers lashed out with beams of hellfire. Nicole swerved left and right dodging the fire as the battle raged around her. Good and bad yokai engaged in a vicious and bloody fight through the streets and in the air. Ryu sparred with oni, dragons lit gashadokuro aflame, and familiar faces aided in her fight. To her right, Nicole sensed Nathan's wingbeats. Even now, during the toughest battle in either of their lives, he too remained steadfast and devoted.

Nicole raced to where the Orochi stood, his giant frame towering over her, and wondered how she would ever be able to defeat him. But no sooner had the thought entered her mind than something odd began to brew inside of her. A vibration in the hilt of the sword sent heat pulsing through her body, and before she knew it, she was growing. By the time the growth stopped, she was twice her original size.

"What the hell?" Nathan asked. Nicole glanced to where he hovered and saw he too had grown.

"It's the spirit of Kushinadahime," Nicole said with a smile.

"She's given us the strength to defeat the Orochi once and for all."

Nicole landed and the earth trembled.

"Your reign is over, Hachi," Nicole said. "You have no hope of winning."

Hachi scoffed. "Nonsense," he said. "Just because you can match me in size doesn't mean you can do so in power."

Nicole heard the sound of Nathan's stinger sliding out of his wrist, and she pointed the blade forward. The Orochi charged, and Nicole and Nathan did the same. She swung her sword at the first head, its teeth gnashing as it aimed for her, and with one swipe, cut it off at the base of the neck. She ducked to avoid another head, then moved forward and slashed at the Orochi's legs, slicing its knee. Behind her, she heard one of the heads wailing. She turned and saw Nathan stabbing it in the eye with his stinger. Greenish-yellow slime oozed from its mouth and nose, and its scales blackened as the head shriveled like a raisin and fell off. Nicole turned and swung her sword down, catching the Orochi's shoulder, and slicing through its wing. She was sprayed by a red mist of blood as thousands of little arteries burst. Hachi screamed and sent another head around her, but Nicole spun in time and stabbed it. The blade pierced the head's throat, causing it to choke and sputter before Nicole thrusted the blade deeper. Blood showered her as the blade exited out the rear of the head and the eyes fell limp.

Nicole backed up and stood beside Nathan, whose stinger was still oozing venom. The Orochi stood injured and bleeding, but before Nicole could think of finishing it off, the heads it had lost grew back like tumorous growths and the creature regenerated the membranes between its wings.

"Not so easy, huh?" Hachi asked.

"Didn't expect to be," Nicole said. She and Nathan charged, and the fight continued. With every swing of the Kusanagi, a head fell, only to be replaced with another. And each time she came close to stabbing the heart, a head would block her. Before long, the ground below them was littered with decapitated

Orochi heads, and its blood coated every surface and flowed through every street like rainwater. And *still* the Orochi refused to fall.

Hachi laughed and gave them a devious glare. "Not even Susanoo could defeat this incarnation of me. No one, not even the wise men of yore, could have predicted how powerful I'd become."

The ground began to shake, and then the heads began to flail like fish and come to life. They turned their dead, glassy eyes to Nicole and Nathan and sprang towards them, mouths wide, teeth dripping with saliva and blood. Nicole fought off the heads as best she could, swinging her blade and catching them in midair, slicing them to ribbons. But they kept coming, swarming them like ants, their jaws snapping as they drew closer.

Overwhelmed, Nicole stood back-to-back with Nathan as the swarm closed in. But before the vile monstrosities could take a chunk out of their scales, they all burst into flame. Nicole looked up and saw Eugenia and Nathan's aunts and uncles fly overhead.

"We'll take care of them," Eugenia said. "You take care of the Orochi."

Nicole nodded and vaulted forward, over the fire and away from the sea of snapping heads. Behind her, below the sound of Nathan's wingbeats, she could hear the high-pitched squeals of the heads as they were burned. Ahead of them, the Orochi was flying towards the coast, and making a beeline to the harbor. Nicole flapped her wings harder, determined to not let Hachi escape her grasp. The gap between them shrank, and she drew close to striking. They were over Tokyo Harbor, and Nicole was so close she could almost touch its tail with the tip of her sword. She gave herself a final push...

Nicole was sprayed by a mist of water, and something very large, and very wet, collided with her. She tumbled to the water below, breaking the surface with a crack that sent jolts of pain through her limbs. Water gushed into her nose and mouth as she tried to stay afloat. She burst from the surface of the water and coughed, and realized that she was no longer holding the Kusanagi. Panicked, she looked around, and caught a glimpse of its blade as it drifted to the bottom of the harbor. Nicole turned to dive in its direction, but something wrapped itself around her neck and pulled her down. Bubbles gushed from her mouth as she was dragged below the surface, the light from above vanishing as her attacker took her further down to the harbor's depths. Nicole clawed at the long, scaly tail that had tightened around her throat, dug her talons into its flesh and ripped, but nothing she did worked. Nicole recalled the ikuchi from earlier, how the creature had been slain by the ryu, and realized that there might have been more hiding in wait.

Larger ones, waiting to attack on Hachi's orders, waiting to trap her.

Nicole's vision blurred, and the world around her faded from view.

CHAPTER 27

Nicole looked out the window of her mother's car, and fought the tug of sleep as Manhattan flashed before her eyes. It was the dead of night, and just a few days after her thirteenth birthday and the beginning of the new year. Her mother spoke, but Nicole hardly noticed. The events of the last few days had left her unable to convey her emotions without crying. All she could think about was her brother, and how he had given her a ring on her birthday.

An engagement ring.

The very thought of it made Nicole's stomach twist in knots, and filled her dreams with ghastly sights and sounds. She hadn't slept since that day, for fear that Lucca might try to spring upon her while she was sleeping, or that her father might grab her and take her away somewhere where no one would find her. It was like living in a nightmare, and even then, Nicole didn't know if what she was seeing now was reality, or a figment of her shattered, sleep-deprived mind.

Chyanne's hands gripped the steering wheel of the BMW her father had gifted her years ago. Her knuckles were white, her eyes red, her brow sweaty. She was wearing her favorite denim jacket, something she had worn for years before Nicole was born. Up ahead, the road was becoming darker and the lights grew few. The road had not been plowed properly, and the car rolled over thick sheets of snow and ice that had accumulated in chunks across the frozen blacktop.

"You have everything?" her mother asked.

"Yeah," Nicole said. She patted a small backpack that sat on the floor between her legs. Of course, she didn't have everything. All of her worldly possessions could not possibly fit in such a small parcel, and by now Nicole assumed she would never see them again. All she had to her name were a few changes of clothes, some notebooks for school, and a calculator. She'd have to stock up on more supplies once she went back to school, but apparently Mr. Allerton knew this and had already started.

"I want to remind you again," her mother said, "these are good people, Nicole. They want to help you, and they want to protect you."

"Why can't you protect me?" Nicole asked.

Her mother paused and choked back tears. "I can't, baby," she said. "Your father is too strong, and if he finds you, there's nothing stopping him from doing what he pleases. This is the only thing I can do to protect you."

"But what's going to happen to you?"

Her mother shook her head. "I don't know, baby, I don't know."

They stopped at the mouth of a tunnel, from which large icicles hung like the teeth of a monster. Two men stood outside, wearing shabby clothes like those of homeless people, waiting for them.

Her mom put the car in park and sighed. "Ready?"

"Yes," Nicole said, but it was a lie. She would never be ready for something like this. She opened the door and made her way towards the tunnel, her boots crunching on ice and salt. The two men approached, and the older of the two held out his hand.

"Hello," he said. "You must be Nicole."

"Yeah," Nicole said, and offered him a gloved hand. The man shook it and gave her a warm smile. "You must be Mr. Allerton."

"Call me Seth," the man said. "And this old fool is Joel. We're happy you're safe and sound."

She felt her mother put her hands on her shoulders. "Now remember, do as they say, and do not try to contact anyone from the Confederacy, not even me."

Nicole turned to face her mother. "But how will I know you're alright?"

Her mother shook her head. "I don't think you will know," she said. "But don't worry about me. This is my mess, and I have to take care of it myself."

Nicole hugged her mother, the worn denim brushing against her face. Her mother returned with a tight embrace, and held her for what felt like forever.

"I love you, mommy."

"I love you, Nicole."

They let go, and her mother took off her jacket.

"What are you doing?" Nicole asked.

"I don't need this anymore," her mother said. "You can have it, but don't wear it to school, and try not to wear it outside. Just put it on when you're in the tunnels and want to remember me."

Nicole took the jacket from her mother, and put it over her winter parka. It was large, too large for her, but she assumed that she would one day grow into it.

Her mother returned to the car. "Goodbye," she said. "If I can come back to you, I will."

"Take care, Chyanne," Joel said. "Please let us know if we can help you."

Her mother took one last look at her, then climbed behind the wheel, turned, and drove off into the night.

CHAPTER 28

Nicole coughed up a lung-full of water and gasped for air. She rolled onto her side and wheezed. When she was finished, she took one final gasp, and opened her eyes. She was on dry land, in the middle of a set of train tracks. She had no idea how she had gotten there, and she couldn't tell how long she had been out, but her scales were drenched.

"Nicole!" she heard Nathan say, before his arms embraced her and nearly squeezed the stuffing from her. Nicole blinked a bit and looked up. Nathan was standing over her, his amber eyes big and worried, his golden scales pale with the trauma of almost losing her. He helped her to her feet.

"What happened?" she asked.

"An ikuchi almost drowned you," Nathan said, "but we saved you."

"*We?*" Nicole asked. It was then when she noticed a figure sitting a few meters behind Nathan. It was a blue-white dragon with her back to them, crouched down next to the decapitated head of the ikuchi. The figure turned her head, and Nicole locked eyes with her mother. Chyanne stood, set the Kusanagi next to the head, and started to walk away.

"Wait," Nicole said, staggering to her feet. She ran over to where her mother stood and put a hand on her shoulder. "You came back."

"I couldn't abandon you again," Chyanne said. "No matter

how much I've failed as a mother. I can't do to you what I did years ago."

"But you didn't abandon me," Nicole said. "You put me in the care of two wonderful people who protected me and nurtured me. And now I'm here, alive and well, all because of you."

Chyanne turned to face Nicole. Her eyes were red with tears, and her scales were pale and sickly. "I understand your anger," Chyanne said, her voice strained. "I did the same thing to my mother years ago. It's the way we Newheart women are, always at odds with one another."

"I'm not angry," Nicole said. "You came looking for me, and that's all that matters."

"But I…"

"You did what you had to do," Nicole said, "and here we are, back together again." Nicole wiped away her mother's tears and picked up the Kusanagi. "Now, want to help me slay an Orochi?"

Chyanne smiled and nodded. "Absolutely."

Nicole saw movement on the horizon, and turned to see the Orochi off in the distance. His back was turned to them, and he was fighting with the allied dragons, who had bathed him in fire that seemed ineffective against his massive form. Nicole stood, sword in hand, with Nathan and her mother on her right and left. Nicole felt the sprits with them as they grew into giants, able to match the Orochi in power and in strength. Nicole spread her wings and took the lead, flying towards the monster with all her might. One of the heads glanced over and noticed them, and made a strange noise that none of the other heads seemed to heed. Nicole winked at the head, swooped, and sliced it clean off.

Hachi looked up, surprised. But his expression quickly turned to malice. "Back for more, or are you here to beg for mercy? Or perhaps you're here to confess your love to me after all."

"Not a chance in hell," Nicole said as Chyanne and Nathan landed beside her, ready to tear Hachi a new one.

"Oh, it's a family reunion," Hachi said, as the decapitated

head grew back again. "More like a funeral! I'll have all three of you wishing for death by the time I'm finished."

"Try us!" Nathan said.

The three of them lunged at the Orochi, who dove towards them in a fury of teeth and fire. Nicole slashed, stabbed, and clawed her way through a shower of blood and scales, trying each step of the way to reach the chest. Finally, she saw an opening in the tangle of heads and necks. She plunged the blade of the Kusanagi into the center of the Orochi's chest, just below the eighth head. Hachi let out a panicked cry and flew into the air while Nicole clung to the hilt. The heads went after Nicole, biting her talons and breathing fire into her face and chest. Nicole wanted to let go, but just as the sensation in her talons had become too unbearable, she felt a jolt from above. She looked up, and saw Nathan on the Orochi's back, his stinger between the Orochi's wings. Hachi let out an ear-splitting cry and all at once, the Orochi grew weak and started to drop. Nathan looked like he was injecting everything he had into the Orochi, the venom spilling out of all eight mouths and its scales rotting away. Nicole tried to hold onto the sword, but her grip grew weaker by the second.

"I got you, baby," Chyanne said. She held Nicole by her shoulders, hoisted her up, and helped her regain her grip. Nicole motioned to Nathan, who let go, and allowed the two to take control. Like a pendulum, Nicole and Chyanne used their weight to force the Orochi down. They plummeted to earth, the Orochi's wings too limp to stop them.

They slammed into the ground, and with their combined momentum, Nicole and Chyanne drove the blade though the Orochi's heart and into the earth beneath it.

"No!" Hachi screamed. "No, it can't be!" A white light emitted from its chest, lighting up the blade and running through both Nicole and Chyanne's veins. "I am the Orochi, feared among the yokai! I can't be defeated by two women!"

"You just were," Nicole said, and forced the blade deeper.

Cracks emerged in the Orochi's scales as the white light

burst from its eyes and mouths. Helpless screams morphed into a single high-pitched squeal. It grew louder and louder until the scales broke away and the light consumed the Orochi.

And then the light faded, and the Orochi had disappeared.

Nicole let go of the sword, still sticking out of the ground, and rolled onto her back. She looked up at the blue sky with a patchwork of clouds and exhaled.

"Is it over?" she gasped.

"Yes."

Nicole rolled over to see Ito sitting nearby. "The soul of the Orochi is forever held inside the Kusanagi. Its threat is no more, and the world is saved."

"Wow," Chyanne said, kneeling next to her daughter. "That was more than I bargained for. Does this mean the yanks aren't going to nuke the city."

Ito nodded. "I'm sure they're aborting their plans as we speak."

Nicole glanced back at the sword. Its white blade was blameless and clean, as though had never seen battle.

She felt Nathan land next to her and he coiled his tail with hers. "How are you feeling?"

"Peachy," Nicole said. "Just peachy."

CHAPTER 29

A few days later, Nicole was called away from the search and rescue operations for a special meeting. She found herself sitting in the back of a Toyota Century, with Ito by her side and the Kusanagi across her lap. She was dressed in a red kimono, on loan from the Tokyo Sanctum. As the car approached the gates to Chiyoda City, she felt a stitch in her chest, and tried putting aside the fact that her host was Naruhito, the Emperor of Japan, who had requested her presence.

The car started down a long, winding road towards the imperial residence, and Nicole checked her reflection again in the drop-down mirror.

"You look fine," Ito said. "The stylist did a fantastic job on your hair and makeup."

"Glad you think so," she said. Nicole sank into the wool seats and stared up at the ceiling of the car.

Whatever, Nicole thought. *Just ignore the fact that he's the head of the oldest hereditary dynasty on earth, whose family legacy stretches back thousands of years. Yeah, just forget that part.*

"We're here," Ito said. "Look sharp."

Nicole straightened herself out and sat up, right as a butler opened the door and held out his hand. She took it, stepped out, and was led up a flight of marble steps to the reception hall of the Imperial Palace. The butler led her and Ito into a waiting room, where they were told Naruhito would join them. The butler left, and Nicole looked around the lavishly decorated room, adorned with ornate pink and white furniture and various artifacts displayed in glass cases along the walls. Nicole gravitated towards a display of katanas, like the one Susanoo wielded centuries ago when the original Orochi was slain.

"What are your plans after all of this is over?" Nicole asked.

"Travel," Ito said. She heard him pull himself up onto a nearby sofa. "Just explore this country from top to bottom. I've spent all my long life cooped up in a cave, and now I want to see all of Japan for myself."

Nicole turned to Ito and smiled. "I think we all deserve a little down time, after all we've experienced."

"What about you?" Ito asked.

Nicole strode towards a woodblock painting of a cherry blossom and pondered the question. "Head back to the states, get a place with Nathan, get my GED. That's what I want to do when I'm done with this adventure."

"That sounds noble," Ito said. "Maybe our paths will cross sometime, hopefully under different circumstances."

Nicole smiled. "Well, if another eight-headed dragon comes thirsting for me, I'll know who to call."

A door at the end of the room opened and Nicole snapped to attention. Naruhito was dressed in a sharp suit and smiled warmly as he entered. He bowed, and both Nicole and Ito returned the gesture.

"Welcome," Naruhito said. "Please, make yourself comfortable."

Nicole sat next to Ito while Naruhito took a seat opposite them.

"To say that I am thankful for your contributions is an understatement," Naruhito said. "You have defeated a monster the likes of which we have not seen in any of our lifetimes."

"I wouldn't have gotten there had it not been for my friends," Nicole said, giving Ito a gentle pat, "and my mother, who for who I am here in her stead."

"It's no issue," Naruhito said. "I am aware of your mother's disdain for politicians, and given her voting record, it may be difficult to get her through security."

Nicole smiled. The thought of her mother having an audience with a literal Emperor was so out of character that it was almost comical.

Nicole noticed the Emperor looking at the sword in her hands, and she placed it on the coffee table between them. Naruhito took it with the tenderness one might have for a newborn and carefully removed it from its scabbard.

"Incredible," he said. "This very sword, forged from the original Orochi, now holds its soul forever." He put it back in its scabbard and admired it thoughtfully. "When I was a young man, my grandfather, Emperor Hirohito, told me that all the legends of dragons and great beasts were just stories. But I held out hope, and continued to believe, even in the face of such doubt and evidence to the contrary." He looked up at Nicole and smiled. "I am not going to hide this sword away. I am going to put it on display, so that generations, young and old, can see it, and marvel."

Nicole nodded. "I think I'm going to miss it," she said. "It felt like a piece of me, but I'm glad you're willing to display it. It deserves to be shown," she gazed down at Ito, "to remind others of the Orochi, and what it represents."

"That even in our darkest hours," Ito said, "love and friendship will conquer all."

❋ ❋ ❋

The airport was deserted, except for the white jet that had flown in from Hawaii to collect Nicole and Nathan. The members of the Tokyo and Seol Sanctums had gathered on the tarmac to wish the Americans goodbye. As their leaders spoke, Nicole hugged her mother with Nathan by her side.

"You sure you don't want to come with us?" she asked.

"Nah," Chyanne said. "I have some loose ends I need to tie in Hong Kong. It shouldn't take me too long, and I'll let you know when I'm ready to go."

"And don't worry," Seth said, "I'll make sure she comes back this time."

Nicole smiled. "I appreciate it," she said. She hugged Seth, and in that moment, Chyanne realized just how much Nicole had grown. Nicole was no longer the girl she had left on the side of the road on a cold winter's night. She was a woman now, with dreams of her own, and damn it if she wasn't going to live them to the fullest.

She glanced at Nathan and nodded. "You take good care of her, you hear?"

"I will, Miss Newheart," Nathan said.

"What did I tell you about surnames?" Chyanne said. "Those are for old people, and I'm barely pushing eighty."

"Is that all?" Seth said. "That's nothing. Wait until you hit a hundred."

"See ya later, old fart," Joel said.

"Get out of the tunnels," Seth jabbed. "Use that money the DC Sanctum gave you for something better, alright."

Daisuke stepped forward and gave Nicole and Nathan hugs. "Come back to visit, why don't you?"

"Of course," Nicole said, buttoning up her denim jacket.

Daisuke patted her on the back and turned to address the rest of the DC Sanctum. As Nicole gathered her things, she stopped and turned to Chyanne.

"Do you want this back?" she asked, gesturing to the jean jacket.

"Nah," Chyanne said. "It looks better on you anyway."

"You sure?" Nicole said. "I always meant to give it back to you when I saw you next."

Chyanne laughed. "It's fine. Keep it. But do me a favor: put that Oui button on it when you get home. I used to keep it on the right sleeve. But took it off after I met your father."

"Okay," Nicole said with a smile. She turned with Nathan

and mounted the steps to the plane. The steps were raised, the plane taxied for the runway, and Chyanne waved as it turned and took off.

"Well, where do you want to start?" Chyanne said to Seth. "You want to catch the first plane to Hong Kong?"

"I say we take it easy for the rest of today," Seth said. "By the way, the last time I was in Tokyo, I went to a sake bar that had some of the best sashimi this side of the Pacific. While I was helping with the search and rescue, I found out that it's still around and owned by the same family." He turned to her. "Why don't we go out for dinner tonight?"

Chyanne giggled. "Are you asking me on a date, Seth Allerton?"

"I don't know," Seth said. "I've never been on one. They weren't invented when I was last in the game."

Chyanne slipped her hand into his. "Well, I think it's time we change that."

They turned and left the airport.

EPILOGUE

Typhoon was sitting atop a glacier in the Arctic Ocean, waiting for his muse, his oracle. He twiddled his toes as snow danced around his face and melted upon contact with his scales. Blue-black waves crashed into the icy formation, spraying him with salt, but his eyes were glued to the spot in the sky where she was supposed to arrive. Typhoon's heart raced as he went through his plan once again. He was positive she would accept, and that she would love the gift he had in store for her. But yet again, he knew there were some gifts he could not grant her. She asked of him more than he was capable of offering, and still others he did not want to give her, no matter how much she asked.

He could never bring himself to kill her, to consume her.

A tear rolled down Typhoon's cheek as he thought of what was to occur. He would be unable to speak to his oracle for some time. It pained him to think of that long of a time. He knew it was wrong of him, but at the same time, he knew his relationship with his oracle was more than just a working one; it was much deeper.

"My dear Naga," Typhoon whispered to the wind. "How I love you so." As far as he was concerned, finding Naga and molding her into the creature she was today was his greatest accomplishment.

A shape appeared in the dark clouds above him, the silhouette of a dragon's wings descending towards the ocean.

Typhoon braced himself as the dragon burst through the clouds and raced over the surface of the water. The waves parted as Naga's wingbeats propelled her towards the glacier. Typhoon marveled at her new form. Her scales were tan around her legs and chest, violet on the ridge of her back, with magenta spikes along her spine and down to the tip of her tail. Her eyes were dark, with red irises that Typhoon knew would glow when needed. When Naga reached the glacier, she flapped her wings up to where Typhoon stood, and landed in front of him.

"I love this form," Naga said with exuberance. "I've never felt so powerful."

"I knew you would," Typhoon said. He embraced her in his arms and held her close.

"I know now what you meant by 'on silent wings'," Naga said. "I never heard my wings flap once."

"Exactly," Typhoon said. "You will move among dragon and human alike without sound, undetected, unheard."

They kissed, and Typhoon felt his scales tingle with a delight he rarely experienced.

"I know I ask of you impossible things," Naga said. "But do me the pleasure of sinking your teeth into my flesh. I want to know the pleasure of pain in this form."

Typhoon smiled. This, at least, was something he could do for her. He opened his mouth wide, revealing his maw full of silver teeth, and sank them into the side of Naga's neck. She gasped, and Typhoon could feel her body relax as her blood filled his mouth and trickled down his throat. He let go, and licked his chops that were stained red, while the wound on Naga's neck evaporated into nothing.

"Gods of men and dragons," Naga exhaled. "I've never felt anything like that before. If only you take a chunk out of me, piece by piece, until there is nothing left except my bones to pick clean."

"But then I would lose my most trusted follower," Typhoon said. "I need you more than anything else in this universe, and now more than ever."

Naga nodded in agreement. He knew she understood it was for the greater good, and that even after everything was said and done and his goals were met, he would still need her to pick up his slack should things go wrong.

"You haven't forgotten my other promise," Typhoon said. "It was hard to do before, but now that we're the same size, I think–"

Naga put a talon on his lips. "I haven't forgotten."

Typhoon wrapped her up in his wings.

❋ ❋ ❋

They left their perch atop the glacier and headed north, towards an icy cove located somewhere in the inhospitable waters of northern Alaska. As they ventured nearer, the skies cleared, and Typhoon could see the dark, crumbling shape of an abandoned oil platform rise from the surface of the ocean. Typhoon slowed as they got closer to the dilapidated structure, whose metal husk was covered in ice and patches of rust that gave no illusions to its condition. They hovered over the long-decommissioned helipad, their wingbeats kicking up clouds of snow and scaring away a colony of nesting birds.

"Lucca!" Typhoon yelled. "Come out!"

The head of a red dragon peered over the edge of the helipad, its face worn, its eyes sleepy. The polar air had done a number on Lucca's figure, leaving him thin, beaten, and leathery. With great pain, Lucca pulled himself up and onto the platform as Typhoon and Naga landed.

"Where the hell have you been?" Lucca snapped. "I've been sitting here on this smelly rust bucket for weeks, freezing my ass off and eating nothing but seagulls waiting for you to come back. What makes you think you can just leave me here to–"

Typhoon smacked Lucca with the back of his hand, and the dragon crumpled.

"I'll make you stay here for the rest of your life if you

don't shut up!" Typhoon regained his composure and gestured to Naga. "Anyway, meet Naga, my oracle. She's come from afar, and you will follow her lead while I am away."

"A woman?" Lucca hissed. "You sent a *woman* to lead *me*? What are you, insane? Salvini men don't take orders from women!"

Naga stepped forward, a wicked grin on her face. "You'll need to make an exception for me," she said. "Typhoon talks through me, speaks through me. I am his second in command, above your father or anyone else in your organization, and from what I recall, you need me more than I need you."

"Every international organization is looking for you," Typhoon said. "The FBI put a bounty on your head, and both the CIA and MI6 are working overtime to find you. If you want to make it out of this with your scales intact, I suggest you show my oracle some respect."

Lucca pulled himself up and sat on his haunches. His face was defiant, but Typhoon could tell in his posture that he had been neutered.

Typhoon turned to Naga. "Remember, I may not be able to speak with you as readily as we used to, but if you need my help, I'll do what I can to assist you."

"That won't be necessary," Naga said. "You've given me all that I need to work in your stead. Do what you need to do, and don't worry about me."

Typhoon smiled. "I knew I could trust you."

"Just come back when it's all over," Naga replied.

Typhoon kissed her again. "Of course," he said. "I'll always be back for you. That is a promise I know I can keep."

They kissed one last time, and Typhoon savored the taste of Naga's lips against his. When they were done, Typhoon gave his wings a single flap, and lifted off the platform, Naga watching with reverence as his figure vanished behind the curtain of clouds.

"Now what?" Lucca asked.

"Let's go somewhere warmer," Naga said. "And the first

order of business when we get to land is simple: you are to give me a foot rub.”

“A foot rub?” Lucca said, disgusted.

“Did I stammer?” Naga asked. “Didn’t think so. Now follow me.”

-The End

ABOUT THE AUTHOR

David Angelo

is an author living and working in the state of Maryland. As of 2025, he has written and self-published six novels, including Scales of Rage: The Dragon Within Book I and Soul of the Prophet: The Elder of Edon book I. He lives with his wife, Linda, their son, Jackson, and their animals.

Connect with him at david-angelo.com

THE DRAGON WITHIN

What if dragons lived among us? What if they appeared human and walked our streets? What if there was a secret conflict that could envelop both our world and theirs?

Two worlds collide as Nathan Van Cleef and Nicole Newheart go to battle against some of the nastiest foes imaginable, in a series that blends fantasy, action, and young adult angst. Scales will fly, streets will burn, and the whole world will never be the same.

Scales Of Rage: The Dragon Within Book I

In a world where mythical dragons live in the shadows of abandoned subway tunnels, Nathan Van Cleef is just trying to survive life as a teenager. Plagued by a mysterious "forever flu" that leaves him bedridden and despondent, Nathan's dreams of a normal life seem as unreachable as the stars. But a series of extraordinary events unveils a secret long hidden within his family—one that thrusts him into a world of ancient sanctums, powerful dragonkin, and deadly adversaries.

On what should be a triumphant graduation day, Nathan's life takes a shocking turn when he's struck by a car and awakens to find scales growing across his body. This startling transformation is just the beginning. As Nathan delves deeper into his family's past, he discovers that his father's legacy is intertwined with the secretive DC Sanctum, a covert group of dragon-human hybrids dedicated to preserving the balance between their two worlds.

With newfound abilities awakening within him, Nathan must navigate a treacherous path filled with fierce battles, ancient grudges, and dark secrets that could threaten everything he holds dear. Allies and enemies emerge from unexpected places, testing Nathan's courage and resolve as he learns to harness the dragon within. From the bustling streets of New York to hidden sanctuaries, Nathan's journey is fraught with peril and wonder.

As Nathan grapples with his own weaknesses and those who wish him harm, he learns that the greatest battles are fought not with claws and fire, but with courage and heart.

Join Nathan on an epic adventure where the lines between myth and reality blur, and destiny awaits those bold enough to embrace the dragon within.

BOOKS BY THIS AUTHOR

Soul Of The Prophet: The Elder Of Edon Book I

Can Harmony Ever Reign Between the Oppressed and the Oppressor?

Embark on an Epic Journey in The Elder of Edon: Soul of the Prophet!

In the mesmerizing world of Edon, where ancient prophecies hold the key to destiny, an unsuspecting teenager, Fin, rises to meet an extraordinary challenge.

Once an orphan cast adrift in the midst of a brutal conflict between the majestic Faranchies and the tyrannical Cullidons, Fin's fate appeared eternally bleak. In the mystical land of dragons, Edon, the Cullidons' oppressive reign shrouded the land in darkness. But when an elder selects Fin to bridge the chasm between the warring dragon races, he faces a monumental decision – to embrace his destiny as the next prophet.

United with an eclectic band of freedom fighters, Fin and his courageous comrades plunge into a perilous odyssey. Together, they confront unimaginable threats and clash with malevolent forces determined to cling to power at any cost. In this relentless struggle against oppression, victory and survival hang precariously in the balance.

Blood Of The Martyrs: The Elder Of Edon Book Ii

Prepare for the Ultimate Showdown in Fin's Fight for Freedom!

A tempest looms on the horizon, and the fate of the Faranchies hangs in the balance.

Join Fin as he leads the charge towards a thrilling apex in the battle for the future of his species!

As the drums of war beat louder, the Children of the Dragon Storm notch their first triumphant victory against the oppressive Parliament. With the taste of success on their lips, Fin and his formidable dragon allies feel unstoppable, believing nothing can thwart their path to liberation. But just as unity between the Faranchies and the Cullidons seems within grasp, an ancient malevolence threatens to tear them apart once more.

From the murky depths of Edon's underworld, Emperor Rixis, fueled by vengeance and aided by the sinister Naga and her lethal cult, Black Moon, devises a sinister scheme to crush Fin and his valiant companions. Their plot, a deadly gambit that could reshape Edon for eternity, spells peril for millions.

As Fin braces for the impending clash, sinister forces encroach upon his world, leaving him exposed and vulnerable. Amidst doubts about the resistance's strategies, tensions escalate, alliances fracture, and the destiny of Edon hangs in the balance.

The enemy grows bolder, shadows deepen, and the sands of time slip away. Can Edon be salvaged, or is it destined to fall into darkness? Prepare for an electrifying saga where every choice carries weight, and the line between victory and defeat blurs with each passing moment!

The Skies Over Lisandra

Unleash the Magic with "The Skies Over Lisandra": A Heart-Stopping Epic of Love, Betrayal, and Redemption

Embark on an exhilarating journey through the enchanted realm of Lisandra, in a captivating tale of love that defies the confines of mortality. This spellbinding saga, from the creative genius behind "Elder of Edon," invites you to plunge into a world brimming with magic, adventure, and the timeless struggle for justice.

Meet Princess Anastasia Roma, whose life of royal privilege spirals into a vortex of betrayal and despair when she's forced into a loveless marriage, only to be cruelly snatched away by death's cold embrace on her wedding day. But death is not the end for Anastasia; it is merely the beginning of her transformation. Reborn as a formidable dragon, she retreats to the solitude of the mountains, guarding her heart and the secrets of the kingdom below.

Isolation shatters with the unexpected arrival of her once baby brother, now a determined warrior with eyes set on the throne usurped by their malevolent uncle Hector. Stirred by ties of blood and the shocking news that her childhood love, Sasha, still lives, Anastasia is thrust into the heart of a rebellion. Alongside Sasha and a mysterious witch, this fearless trio embarks on a quest to overthrow tyranny and restore peace to their fractured homeland.

However, the winds of fate are unpredictable. The appearance of Typhoon, a charismatic dragon with intentions as mysterious as his origins, presents Anastasia with choices that blur the lines between right and wrong, passion and duty. In this tumultuous realm, alliances are fragile, and the quest for power is fraught with peril.

"The Skies Over Lisandra" is a riveting exploration of the enduring bonds that tie us, the sacrifices made in the name of love, and the courage to confront the past to forge a new destiny. Prepare to be whisked away on an unforgettable adventure where dragons soar high, magic reigns supreme, and the flames of love burn eternal.

Perfect for fans thirsting for a new classic in the fantasy genre, "The Skies Over Lisandra" promises a journey of epic proportions. With every turn of the page, discover the power of love reborn and the indomitable will to reclaim what was lost. This is your next fantasy fixation, a dazzling story that captures the heart and imagination, proving once and for all that true love never dies—it is reborn.